Rockland Point
Revelations

Dave Metcalf

ISBN: 1987735757
ISBN-13: 9781987735758

ACKNOWLEDGEMENTS

This book bears my name, but would not have seen the light of day if not for some very special people.

Thanks to my wife, Sandra, who gave me valuable feedback by proofreading each chapter as it came off the printer.

I am grateful to my son, Keith and his wife Kathy and their daughter Emma, in their home where the cover was created.

Thanks to the leader of Englewood Authors, Ed Ellis, who gave me hands- on help throughout the publication process. I owe a shout out to my fellow writers of Englewood Authors who gave me their support and much-appreciated advice as I read my chapters in group meetings.

From my past, I must acknowledge my fifth-grade teacher David Cantwell and high school English teacher Arthur Bennett. They told me I had a talent for writing and encouraged me to pursue the craft, which I did, beginning with a 25- year newspaper career.

Saving the best for last, I express my love and gratitude to my late parents, Ralph and Alice Metcalf, who raised me in Dartmouth, Massachusetts, which, not by coincidence, is a coastal town very much like Rockland Point.

ROCKLAND POINT REVELATIONS

This story begins someplace along the
Atlantic seaboard in a sleepy coastal
Massachusetts town.

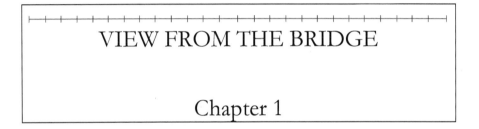

VIEW FROM THE BRIDGE

Chapter 1

Manny DeMello, with a rare day off from his trade as a day laborer, part-time landscaper and fix-it specialist, was fishing off the Smith Neck Harbor Bridge on an unusually warm summer day. To his left, to his right and on the side of the bridge behind him were a total of 15 or 20 others. Manny and the others were treating themselves to a popular local past-time: Dropping a line off the bridge over the waist-high railing to the water about 20 feet below.

The bridge was also the perfect vantage point to view what the locals called "The Island Lights." The lights appeared at night in the warm weather months over Forbes Island, which was approximately four miles past the harbor out to sea. But there was no predicting when the lights, which showed for only a few moments, would appear; some years they did not appear at all, sometimes they would show several days in a row, other times they would show an average of once every couple of weeks.

The island spectacle consisted of bouncing balls of light one could fantasize were being juggled by a pair of huge invisible hands.

For as long as anyone can remember, Manny, whose full name was Manuel Antonio Souza DeMello, hired himself out for construction projects that involved new homes, buildings for newly-established businesses, home improvements, land-clearing efforts and the like. He was not a licensed electrician or plumber, but he could use wood, metal, screws, nails and power tools to build or fix just about anything. And he did all this and other things to make a comfortable living in Rockland Point.

It seemed the only time anybody in town saw Manny was when he was fishing off the bridge or working. Manny wanted it that way.

In the summer months, Manny, now in his 60s and a town resident for nobody knows exactly how long, also had a client list for lawn mowing, tree trimming and any other kind of yard work. In the winter months, when construction projects were pretty much on hold, he could be seen working as a school and church custodian or plowing or shoveling snow. He basically took any employment he could get.

He and his wife Maria lived in the outskirts of town. They had neighbors, but the closest one was a half mile or so from their one-story natural shingle house, which sat on a perfectly manicured quarter acre.

The DeMellos were friendly to all with whom they came in contact. They were two of the many Portuguese living in Rockland Point. Like many of the other Portuguese in town, Manny and Maria proudly and often traced their ancestry back several generations to commercial fishermen and whalers from the Azores, who eventually settled with their families in fishing ports along the east coast. Their forbearers, each claimed, fell in love with coastal Massachusetts and stayed.

Among fellow townsfolk who knew the DeMellos were 20 something's Alex Bean and Woody Engle. This day they ambled alongside Manny on the bridge.

"Any luck today, Manny?" Alex asked as Manny stared straight ahead toward Forbes Island as he held his fishing pole in his weather-worn, muscular and heavily callused hands. Without turning, he gave a grin of recognition from a face that was bronzed and deeply wrinkled from too many years out in the sun without the benefit of sun block, and from his chain smoking days, which he liberated himself from cold turkey about five years before.

"Hey. How you guys been? Great to see you. They don't seem to be biting today," Manny answered. "But what's better on a day off than to dangle a line into the water?"

The bridge was a short span connecting two bodies of land and had a daily visit from locals and non-locals during the warm-weather months. Manny got to know them all over the years; the men and women fishing, the daily joggers, the gossipers, the millionaires, factory workers, doctors, lawyers and the occasional celebrity from TV or Hollywood. Those celebrities, along with wealthy retirees, considered Rockland Point a vacation destination and most of them lived in one of the town's two upscale gated communities.

But regardless where they lived in or near town, everybody on the bridge at any given time would mingle and chat without regard for one another's station in life.

One of the local mysteries involved those who came from as much as 40 miles away just to drop a line off this particular bridge, despite the fact there were perhaps hundreds of similar leisurely fishing spots in this section of the state.

The big question was always, "Why Rockland Point?" although nobody ever seemed to search for an answer.

"I think I just got a hit," said Manny, as he jerked his pole to set the hook on what would often be some small fish species. This time Manny hooked what the locals called a choggie, about six inches long and perhaps best used as bait for bigger prey.

"Would you look at that monster?" teased Woody.

The diversity on the bridge mirrored the relationship between Alex and Woody. Alex, around 6' 5" (a good foot taller than Manny) and always dressed neat as a pin, was a reporter for the nearby Deermont Times. He was a skeptic, although not a cynic, and liked to have things explained to him.

Woody was just less than 5' 11", pudgy, a budding actor and didn't care all that much about how people felt about his sometimes mismatched wardrobe. He was affable with everybody. It was suggested to him more than once that he join Weight Watchers.

Alex was about to drop a line into the slightly choppy water but stopped when the air and everyone's conversations were invaded by the sudden obnoxious blast of an air horn. It was blared by the bridge tender to signal the on-the-hour opening of the swing bridge section in the middle of the span to allow passage of pleasure boats with high masts to the other side. Those boats, moored on one side or the other of the bridge, created two-way traffic between the otherwise landlocked bay and the open harbor which eventually opened to the Atlantic Ocean.

Everybody on the mechanized platform had to reel in their lines, pick up their bait buckets and any fish they may have hooked. They were not allowed on the humpback span when it was swung to a 90 degree angle. They had to move to the stationary portions of the bridge that were a mere few feet above water level and switch from dropping a line to casting it.

Going over the bridge from what most locals called "the village" to the other side took about 45 seconds by car due to the speed limit, and maybe just over a minute by bike. There was a land route from the village to the other side which involved a detour of approximately four miles.

The bridge was built as a totally wooden structure in the late 1800s. Now it was concrete reinforced and, of course, partially mechanized.

"We're coming back out here at sunset tonight," Alex said to Woody and Manny as they sauntered off the soon-to-be-moving span. "Sandra says she likes seeing the island lights. And besides, husbands and wives should spend leisure time together in romantic settings. At least that's what she tells me."

"Well, Barbara and I will be out here with you tonight," Woody said. "She's always telling me about husbands and wives being in a romantic setting once in a while. Although I'm not sure where this bridge and the island lights, if we see them, fall on the romantic evening scale of one to ten.

"And don't forget the bug spray. The mosquitoes can be torture. Hey, want to join us, Manny? You and your wife."

"Thanks lots for the invite," Manny said. "But there's groundbreaking on a mini-mall near Horseneck Acres tomorrow and I'm on the crew. Gotta be there for 5 a.m. But I would like to join you guys sometime to watch the lights."

"The island lights may never be explained well enough for me," Alex said. "I know they are a local legend appearing over Forbes Island sporadically, and mostly on warm summer nights and for a few minutes, if that. But what the heck? An atmospheric anomaly? That's bullticky as far as I'm concerned because they appear only over the island."

"So what are they, Mr. Newspaperman? Maybe a mini version of the Northern Lights, aurora borealis?" Woody asked.

"I don't know, Mr. Leading man. To me, the phrase 'atmospheric anomaly' needs some more explaining," Alex said. "But UFO? Alien visitors? Of course not. What do you think, Manny?"

Manny quickly glanced skyward, took a deep breath, and then looked at the ground. "I really have to go," he said. "See you guys later."

Since he had parked on the far side of the bridge, in the boat launch parking lot instead of on the village side, he didn't have to wait for the swing bridge to close. He was able to walk to his work truck and drive off toward home.

The bed of Manny's pickup carried a large, shiny tool box, a step ladder and some five-gallon buckets. There were also a shovel and a rake braced ramrod straight, almost proudly, against the back of the truck's cab. Definitely it was a working man's truck.

"It's almost like he bolted like a bat out of heck," Woody said with an inflection of confusion as they watched Manny's truck shrink into the distance along Bay View Road. "We started talking about the island lights, and boom, he suddenly had to leave."

"You need to chill, Woody. There's nothing weird in him leaving suddenly," Alex said. "Remember, it is near supper time and he probably wants to get some meaningful shut-eye before he reports to work at 5 a.m. You know, that time of the morning when the rest of us are sawing off some Z's?"

But there would come a time when Alex would want to have a serious chat with Manny.

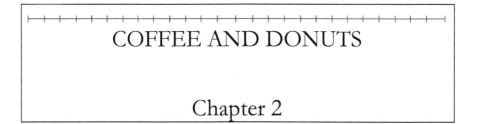

COFFEE AND DONUTS

Chapter 2

"You don't think the time we spent last night at the bridge was a waste, do you, Alex?" his wife Sandra asked at the breakfast table.

Alex Bean gently put up his left hand in a gesture of asking for a few seconds to allow him to finish off the last forkful of scrambled egg before answering. "No, not at all. We didn't see the island lights, but the mosquitoes and no-see-ums apparently didn't see us and stayed away from the bridge."

"It wasn't a waste for me, either," she said. "We got to listen to Woody brag about the play he is going to be in at Horseneck Playhouse with Tom Cruise's cousin, and I got a couple of good recipes from Barbara. Woody and Barbara giggled a lot, too. You know, they've been married about three years and they still act like a couple of crazy kids."

"Speaking of kids, Sandra, when do you think they will be adding to the Engle family?"

"Not sure, but as soon as Barbara mentions she's expecting and tells me not to tell anybody yet, I'll let you know right away," Sandra said with a wink and a grin.

"By the way, Sandra dearest, those recipes you say you got from Barbara - are they for home consumption or for the business?"

"For the shop. Barbara and I have owned that place for two years now, and we think it's about time we did something with the menu. It's a coffee shop with donuts, sandwiches, soup, salad and pastries. We need to make it a coffee shop with a lot more than that on the menu."

"I know business isn't so hot lately," Alex said. "Why? Is it because people aren't so crazy anymore about sandwiches, soup and salad?"

"No, Alex. It's because people are coming in for a cup of our gourmet coffee and maybe a donut and nothing else. We have toyed with the idea of changing the name of the shop from 'The Village Grind' to 'Heaven by the Bridge' if that will help. After all, it is at the foot of the bridge and the village regulars come by for coffee and sometimes a bite. But we need more."

"Well, Sandra, I'm on a two-week vacation from the newspaper and Woody has a week off from his day job at the Home Depot warehouse, so if you girls need any help with the changes at the coffee shop, let us know."

Sandra's face adopted a pensive aura. It was as if she didn't hear Alex. She spoke: "Maybe we could run some elaborate ads on local radio and TV and get some well-known locals to do testimonials about our shop. People like Hamilton Forbes. He's always coming in, usually just for coffee, though."

Hamilton T. Forbes, a multi-millionaire, became a widower prior to moving to Rockland Point about 15 years before from his native Virginia. He steadfastly kept details of his wife's death private and most of the townspeople respected that, never seeking details. Hamilton was a philanthropist whose generosity created baseball and softball fields, tennis courts, soccer fields and basketball courts for the town's youth and adults.

He also purchased land and sold it to the town for one dollar on the condition it be used for the construction of a new library and a senior center, both to be handicapped accessible. When the town council agreed, he presented the body a hefty check to defray some of the constructions costs.

"I'm sure he would go along with that radio ad," Alex said. "If it helps the local economy, he's for it, or so it seems."

"Our struggle at the shop is tough to figure, though," Sandra said, literally scratching her head. "The coffee shop occupies one of the prime retail locations in the village. Anybody walking on to or off the bridge at our end of the span has to walk by the coffee shop or directly across the street from it. The parking lot holds only eight cars, but that's not the problem. That part of the village is alive with foot traffic, especially in the spring and summer.

"So why is the coffee shop struggling?"

"You're right, good question," Alex said. "Business was booming for a long time after you girls bought it."

The Forbes family legacy was built primarily on real estate, beginning in their native Virginia, or so the local narrative went. When Sandra and Barbara bought the lot for the donut shop, Hamilton called Mrs. Bean to wish her and Barbara well. He told them, not jokingly, he wished he had bought the place because of its retail potential.

So what happened?

Hamilton, in his early 40s and living alone, was easy to spot around town. He never wore shirts loose enough to deemphasize his pot belly. He also seemed to never clean his eye glasses after they were spotted by the salt water spray kicked up by his skiff on trips to and from Smith Neck Harbor and Forbes Island, that bit of land a few miles beyond the harbor.

The rest of the 6-foot-4 of him, though, was positive.

His ever-present smile matched up well with this eyes which were a shade of blue that invited women to flirt. He also possessed a handsome nose and chin straight out of some classic Greek art. It was all topped by shocks of curly brown hair tumbling out from under his New York Yankees baseball cap. That headgear started more than one baseball debate, usually good natured, between him and the staunch Red Sox boosters among the locals.

Hamilton and his two siblings, a younger sister in Washington State and an older brother in Utah, were all that remained of the Forbes clan. Forbes Island was purchased by the family in the early 1900s. Hamilton was now in charge of it.

Under the auspices of persons operating behind the scenes, he was also charged with the care of at least two properties on the mainland of the town: A house, which dated back to the colonial days, on Prospect Street near the bay; and a former school house on Russell Road he converted into an art gallery. The latter was a two-story stone and shingle structure whose backyard was intriguing - the once grassy, spacious school playground was now overgrown with trees and bushes.

On those times Hamilton stopped by The Village Grind he often left a large tip, even if he ordered only coffee, then drove over the bridge to the boat launch area. He would do the pre-launch check on his Boston Whaler skiff while having pleasant chat with other boaters, then head out to Forbes Island. He was seldom asked why he went there. It was common knowledge he owned it.

The people in town knew that was normally his boating destination because he could be seen as he and his skiff, which could carry three or four people safely, left Smith Neck Harbor to the open Atlantic Ocean. The island was the only open ocean land he could possibly reach in a small boat with small fuel capacity. And the port side of his skiff carried a "Forbes Island or Bust" sign. He occasionally ferried townsfolk to the island just for the heck of it and a quick tour of the 30-acre island via all-terrain vehicles. They all reported the island was desolate, except for small game such as rabbits.

One place Hamilton, under strict orders, never took visitors was the part of the island where there was a clearing just large enough to accommodate a helicopter. A hundred yards or so beyond the clearing was a nondescript, neatly-kept three-room windowless cabin. Due to a high curtain of dense vegetation and unique natural lay of the land, plus a thick natural canopy of tree tops camouflaging it from above, the cabin would be visible only when one was pretty much there.

And getting there was virtually impossible unless a person knew which paths to take to avoid large pools of deadly quicksand and water channels that were about 10 feet deep and a habitat for venomous snakes. But anybody who was not one of the handful of people who knew the safe route, and innocently ventured anywhere near the cabin, would be greatly discouraged by a laborious trek through muck and marsh land that would make the most intrepid explorer give up and turn around.

Fortunately, there was never any indication of lamentable accidents, fatal or otherwise, involving the quicksand and makeshift moats. Thus Hamilton was confident the cabin's existence was known only to him and the select handful of others. And some of those others knew nothing more about Rockland Point than its location on a map.

Hamilton seldom utilized the cabin, even though it had a bed, desk, table and chairs and a couch.

A generator about the size of a mini fridge stood outside the cabin's back door under a canopy. Mounted just under the canopy was a state of the art security camera pointed at the door of a nearby shed.

Part of his assignment was to keep close tabs on what this security camera and others revealed on the island and elsewhere.

ON WITH THE SHOW

Chapter 3

Manny knew the cabin's location well, and went there whenever Hamilton told him to. Manny's cell phone would ring any time 24/7 and he would be told, by an automated female voice, what day and time to be at the island cabin.

That automated voice simply spoke a three-digit number tied to an ever changing code system to impart the information Manny needed, and then hung up. Since he was an independent contractor, he could set his own mainland work schedule and not draw suspicion when he left a work site at any time.

Sometimes he was needed at the cabin within hours, and sometimes in a day or two. The phone message speaking only a random number, and in a female voice, was meant to keep a secret hidden in plain sight.

"Oh, Maria. I need to find my windbreaker in case I have to go to the cabin tonight. Kind of chilly for this time of year," Manny said to his wife, who was in the kitchen of their house, preparing lunch.

"Your jacket is on the back of the couch, Manny. I think you put it there yourself when you picked up your mail I put there this afternoon. Remember? After you got back from your temp job at the mini-mall ground breaking near Horseneck Acres?"

"Oh, yes. I was about to read my mail, but got distracted by the soccer game on the television and never opened it."

"Well, Manny. You should have opened your mail. I think there was something there from the chief."

Manny rifled through the four or five sticks of mail and came across what he was looking for, what Maria told him was there.

There it was. A certified letter addressed to 'Manuel DeMello, 1076 Bakerville Road, Rockland Point, Massachusetts', with the return address of 'Luxury Time Share Central, PO Box 4526, Wingarde, Louisiana'.

He opened it.

"How come you didn't open it, Maria? You're an agent with a high-level clearance just like me."

"I just got busy, just like you," she replied in a friendly mocking tone.

The certified letter, in code, read:

"We were able to secure some open weeks in several time share condos around the country to cover a period of the next 18 months or so. We are happy to hear you are interested in a time share located near the lake you mentioned in our last communication. We also thought you might have plans to travel through the mountains we displayed in our catalogue of April of this year. There are time shares available in that area, too. We suggest you book early, since that area is tremendously popular."

———————————————————

The message in code was clear to the Portuguese couple - They were to begin preparing two properties in Rockland Point. One was the house on Prospect Street, identified as 'near the lake' and the other was the two-story art gallery's grounds, or 'through the mountains' that was once a play area for the school that was converted into the gallery. The Prospect Street house had a secret passage accessed in the basement. It was a tunnel leading to a concealed area by the bay. The grounds in back of the art gallery, when it was a grade school, had a couple of softball fields, a soccer pitch and a spacious general play area. Now those grounds were overgrown, perfect for concealing a massive cleared out underground area.

The DeMellos and Hamilton were the only people in town who had knowledge of the passage to the bay and the expansive underground space.

There was to be some activity in those two locations in the not too distant future, the letter's code implied.

"Well, Manny, until those two areas are ready for their intended purpose, we need to keep the public focused on the island lights. The chief is sending up a meteorologist to talk up the island lights as an atmospheric anomaly, and I think that's a great idea. He'll, quote - show up - unquote, on the bridge on a given night when the lights are going to show. He'll pretend to be surprised when the lights appear and start talking it up with the townsfolk there, show his credentials as a member of a federal atmospheric council and convince them it is a phenomenon of the atmosphere."

"That's nice deception, Maria. That way the talk around town will be about the island lights and scant attention will be paid to what's going on Prospect Street and at the art gallery. Just some people working there; home improvements, land clearing. And what we're really doing is all hidden in plain sight."

The couple was used to being in and around an atmosphere of deception, dealing with spreading disinformation when citizens apparently have evidence of things like UFOs and time travel.

Manny's cell phone rang.

He got the message and replaced the phone in the holster on his tool belt. "The only thing we're going to deal with for now is the island," he told his wife. "I'm going there tomorrow night. Must mean the light show is on. Anybody who shows up at the bridge will get an eyeful. And also hear from that meteorologist the chief will be sending up."

Manny and Maria failed to consider that people in town could still ask questions. Some of which would be difficult to safely answer.

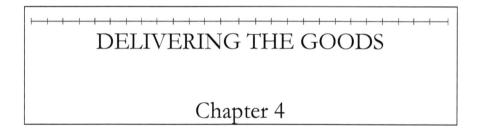

DELIVERING THE GOODS

Chapter 4

Everything was in place. The material to be disposed of on Forbes Island was on the last leg of its journey by a helicopter which would land in the island clearing at precisely 10:08 p.m. It would be comfortably after dark by then as gawkers on the Smith Neck Harbor bridge would be waiting for the appearance, or non appearance, of the island lights.

The helicopter had night friendly instrumentation and a sound abatement system which made it virtually undetectable in flight at night. It could land on Forbes Island on its mission and not be seen or heard by people on the bridge, even on a calm, peaceful warm summer evening when sound could carry great distances. Any incidental light the chopper might emit during its landing phase would be hidden in plain sight, behind the island lights.

"Check your instruments, Horace," the helicopter pilot said to his flight companion.

"All set, Marwell," was the reply. "I received the 'Ready' pulse on the control panel from Manny in the shed next to the cabin. No vessel within the zone of concern and the landing area is ready to receive us."

"Thanks, Horace. We'll be able to land safely and carry the material to the shed. Then Manny can start the bobbing lights so the disposal process can begin hidden behind them. "

On the bridge with the sight-seers this night was the man claiming to be a meteorologist who just happened to be in town for a couple of days.

Sticking with the covert plan, he claimed to have seen the island lights a few times over the years. He started to chat it up with people on the span, casually identifying himself and telling them he knew the lights were an atmospheric anomaly.

"Not ball lightning, though," he said in a scholarly tone of voice to all within earshot. "Ball lightning can be red, orange, and yellow. These lights are white and apparently always spherical. But ball lightning varies in shape between rods, ovals and only sometimes spherical."

He added: "Ball lightning is generally considered to appear in association with the more common cloud to ground lightning. The strange thing, though. Science didn't even validate the existence of ball lighting until the 1960s."

He had done his job. The talk around town for the next several days would be about his mini-lecture on the island lights. Some would accept his interpretation of the unfolding events, while others would disagree with the whole ball lightning-atmospheric anomaly thing.

With the focus thus, work on two other covert projects in Rockland Point could proceed relatively unnoticed.

The helicopter landed undetected amid the island lights, which were entertaining to the gawkers on the bridge.

"How was the trip?" Manny, after running into the clearing from his duties in the shed, asked the pilot. The Portuguese handyman began peeling off gray, stringy residue from his bright yellow jumpsuit.

"Not bad at all," Marwell replied. "The plane flight from Area 51 in Nevada to Virginia was a tad bumpy, but the transfer of material to the helicopter went smooth as butter on silk – again. Another load for disposal. We'll give you a hand."

Manny, Horace and Marwell spent the next several minutes toting 15 seven-foot high cylindrical transparent plastic teleportation tubes to the door to the shed for disposal. The tubes, large enough to accommodate one man, had bits of scorched wire as well holes that once held dials and other instruments.

The tubes were light as the proverbial feather, but awkward to carry.

"You guys go put the camouflage vegetation on the helicopter and bed down in the cabin as usual," Manny said. "There are some MREs there. Thank goodness the military invented meals ready to eat.

"There will be some extra thick fog around here tomorrow, as usual after a delivery by you guys, so you can instrument fly out of this place undetected."

Manny took the tubes, one by one, through the shed door, turned to his left and went down seven steps. When all 15 tubes were at the bottom of the stairwell, he placed them singly and upright into what could be described as a walk-in closet.

He then backed out. As he did so, he mentally counted the tubes he had placed in the compartment, closed that door, sidled to his left two steps and flipped two ordinary-looking wall switches. The tubes, made of a plastic material the outside world knew nothing about, incinerated and the light-emitting vapors escaped through a vent on the shed's roof. Of course it was all disguised by the bobbing island lights Manny had activated.

The crowd on the bridge let out the oooohs and aaahs for the light show. Some even applauded. A few moments, the show was over and everybody headed for home.

And so did Manny. He didn't bother changing out of his teleportation jumpsuit as he stepped into another closet-like door in the shed's basement. He pushed a few buttons, and within seconds he was in the basement of his home, a good five miles from the island.

Hamilton T. Forbes, in the study of his mansion at Mishaum Shores, made a check mark in a notebook and placed it back into his shirt breast pocket. He had watched a live feed from the security camera on the cabin as the three men carried exactly 15 teleportation tubes the door of the shed. Manny was the only one who entered the shed.

Maria welcomed her husband home, helped him out of his yellow jumpsuit and punched in a five-digit code on a wall-mounted number pad to signal Hamilton that another leg of the latest mission was complete.

Manny climbed into bed, kissed his wife good night, turned off his bedside table lamp and ran down a mental checklist. That list included all the steps to get the fog machine up and running the next morning so the helicopter could take off from the island undetected.

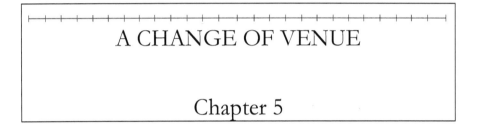

A CHANGE OF VENUE

Chapter 5

The day dawned cloudless, the sun soon glinting delicately off the tops of miniscule waves that lapped gently on the sides of the hundred or so pleasure boats moored for the summer in Smith Neck Harbor.

The harbor was filled with playthings of the wealthy, which flocked to the coastal Massachusetts town of Rockland Point in the warm weather months.

These annual visitors did clog the streets of the town and make parking spaces a precious commodity, restaurant reservations suddenly mandatory, and foot traffic in the village portion of the town a downright nuisance. All this sometimes irked the locals, who the remainder of the year could park virtually anywhere and walk into any business in town without having to jostle through a crowd.

But the bed and breakfasts, motels, eateries, various businesses of all sizes, and even kids with lemonade stands came to appreciate the influx of money. It helped bolster the local economy and put a lid on local taxes.

"Did you see the fog roll in out by the island this morning?" Alex Bean said to his wife Sandra, who was behind the counter of 'The Village Grind' coffee shop she co-owned with close friend Barbara.

"Yes. It came on all of a sudden," Sandra answered. "It was almost like somebody threw a curtain up in front of the island."

Barbara, wiping her flour-speckled hands on her apron, entered the coffee shop's retail area, brushing aside the hanging cloth door that separated the front of the shop from the bakery ovens and donut racks in the back.

"It's happened before," she said, having overheard the Beans' discussion. "It gets real foggy suddenly by the island, but nowhere else. Then it all clears up."

Alex cupped his chin in his hand and tilted his head to one side. His furrowed brow and shifting eyes indicated he was processing what he had just heard and waiting for a mental readout.

"You know what?" he offered. "We've all seen that sudden appearance and then disappearance of the morning fog. And you know what else? I have to tell you this may sound crazy, but the fog like we saw a couple of hours ago, as far as I can recollect, always - and I mean always - comes the morning after the island lights appear."

Sandra hopped behind the cash register and Barbara returned to her baking duties in the back of the shop as customers began to pop in. Alex smiled and waved to his wife and blew her a kiss as he left The Village Grind, and walked onto the bridge.

Alex's journalistic curiosity kicked in, even though he was on vacation. That used to upset him, until one day he realized finding answers caused him to relax.

He was a few yards onto the bridge when he felt a shoulder poke from behind. That's the way his life-long friend Woody Engle often greeted him. Irritating? Yes. But Alex knew it would never change, and he did not want anything to interfere with their friendship.

"What's that bee in your bonnet?" Woody asked his pal, sensing Alex was deep in thought.

They walked to the bridge's waist-high railing, rested their elbows on it and each clasped his hands in front of him, almost in an attitude of prayer. They both stared toward the island.

"Something does not add up," Alex said. "The fog always appears the morning after the lights appear. And there's one other thing that bugs me."

There was silence as Alex gazed upward, inhaled and sighed deeply, slowly shaking his head as if there was something he needed to say but wished he did not have to.

"Out with it," Woody pleaded, knowing something productive was going on inside Alex's head. They had been inseparable friends since about 20 years ago in kindergarten. They knew each other's body language.

"Well," Alex began as he glanced all around him to be sure they were alone enough so he could at least whisper without being overheard. A few others were on the bridge, but well out of earshot.

"Did you ever notice this, Woody?" Alex asked, barely above a whisper. "I mean did it ever occur to you in all the perhaps hundreds of times we have been on this bridge to watch the island lights? It just struck me."

Woody then whispered his reply. "Please, Alex. I am planning on a career as an actor, not a mind reader."

"Well," Alex began again. "I have never seen Manny on the bridge on the nights when the lights did appear. I'm as sorry as I can be, but it seems much too much of a coincidence to me. He's right next to us, watching with everybody else on the nights when we see no island lights. Then - poof - the lights appear one night, but there is no Manny."

"Maybe we just didn't see him, Alex."

"I don't buy that. That can't be the case. He always seeks us out. This has me stumped. Call it a journalist's nose for news, a newsman's gut feeling. Call it whatever. I suspect something. Clandestine? That's too weird. But...circumstances just don't add up in my mind."

Woody put his hand on his best buddy's shoulder and whispered forcefully through clenched teeth. It had the tone of a lecture. "OK, Alex. You are starting to freak me out. Be honest with me. Are you talking some Twilight Zone scenario? Like Manny has something to do with the island lights? That's why he isn't here when they do appear? And the fog..."

"Stop right there Woody. I just don't know. I just don't know. I guess I'll just, the next time I run into him, ask him point blank what's going on. Maybe I am reading too much into this, maybe it's nothing. But I need to know so I can get this nagging doubt out of my mind."

"Oh, nice play, Shakespeare," Woody replied with a heavy dose of sarcastic disappointment. "You mean to tell me that you, my BFF, have been dwelling on this for who knows how long and this is the first I am hearing about it?"

"I would have told you about it before, but I needed to be sure my suspicions had a firm foundation."

Neither Alex nor Woody, nor anybody else in Rockland Point would see the island lights again.

Manny, out on the island a few hours before, checked his dials and manual controls as he sent the 'Ready' pulse signal to the departing helicopter. The fog he had activated cloaked the helicopter from view from the mainland and any nearby vessels and it flew to its home base, its location unknown even to Manny.

The Portuguese handyman grabbed a sealed letter-size envelope off a shelf in the shed where he had been manning the light and fog controls over the past 12 or so hours, with some sleep time in between.

The envelope had been given to him by the helicopter pilot with instructions to open it when the chopper flew off the island. Manny always followed instructions.

He opened the envelope, read the paper inside, then wadded the paper with angry hands, ripped it to pieces, slammed the shreds to the ground and stomped on them.

The paper, in code, informed Manny the island operation - the disposal of the teleportation tubes, the island lights that masked the arrival of the helicopter and the tubes' disposal, the fog to cover the aircraft's departure - was to cease immediately. He took fierce pride in his work, no matter the task, and became upset when his work was assigned to the wayside.

Manny donned a yellow jump suit, stepped into the shed's teleportation chamber and seconds later was in the basement of his home on the mainland.

"It finally happened, Maria," he said to his wife, who helped him out of the jumpsuit. Manny was trembling and speaking loudly and animatedly with anger.

"No more plastic teleportation tubes. The island operation is shut down. All that work I did over the years on the cabin, the shed, maintaining the controls to activate the lights and the fog, setting up and maintaining the surveillance camera for Hamilton to oversee everything."

"Well," Maria responded softly in a successful attempt to calm her husband. "We both knew this part of the operation would come to an end someday. No more helicopter deliveries, or need for the cabin, the shed, surveillance camera, booby trap landscape. And you did mention the portable teleportation tubes were to become a thing of the past as soon as the stationary booth method was developed to perfection."

"You're right, I know," Manny spoke slower now, his shakes of anger gone. "I volunteered to be the guinea pig for the development of the booth transfer method. That's how I get to the island shed to here and back to the island in seconds. Nothing needs to be disposed of. Only hidden. I just put on that yellow jumpsuit, open the panel that looks like a run of the mill circuit breaker box in anybody's basement, flip a switch or two and transport."

Manny broke into a smile on his weather worn, wrinkled, handyman face. "You know? There were a few times I flipped that teleportation switch and found myself mouthing the phrase 'Beam me up, Scotty.'"

Maria reached out with loving compassion and stroked her husband's head of thick, black hair, her demeanor telling him she shared his disappointment in the closing of the island operation.

But the couple knew this was not the end of anything. It was only the beginning.

INVESTIGATION UNDERWAY

Chapter 6

Manny put his handyman skills to work on a busy morning on Forbes Island. He closed up shop, so to speak, since that venue had served its purpose in the covert operations just off the mainland of Rockland Point. The teleportation tubes, which had been routinely disposed of there, were now officially replaced program-wide by new technology.

On the island this morning, he drained all the now-unnecessary security moats which were in close proximity to the hidden cabin and adjacent shed and poisoned the snakes that inhabited the moats. He neutralized the deadly quicksand in the clandestine area with a concoction of cement and a specially formulated substance akin to kitty litter.

He also removed and destroyed all tell-tale devices, surveillance cameras, switches, and mechanized objects involved in the destruction of the teleportation tubes and the island lights and morning-after fog activation that once masked the departure of helicopters in the covert operation. The cabin and shed, now safely accessible to all, would appear to invitees and interlopers as structures which were simply there, obviously the property of one Mr. Hamilton Forbes, whose family owned the island.

A few years ago, Manny was ordered to field test the latest teleportation technology. Despite the tearful pleas of his wife to beg off the project, he tested it successfully.

The only scare came on his second try when he flipped a couple of switches and passed out, triggering an automatic shutdown of that teleportation attempt. That physical anomaly was traced to a diabetic reaction on a day when he failed to follow his doctor-ordered regimen due to his focus on the project at hand. He came to, quickly - no harm, no foul - and he has since stuck to his medical needs religiously.

The new teleportation method began with the donning of a magnetized yellow jumpsuit which was wired with a sophisticated GPS woven into the fabric. He would then step into an air-tight broom closet-size room, flip a switch or two on what looked like a normal circuit breaker box on the wall. A few seconds later, he would be at a pre-determined site, sometimes miles away.

Manny was one of only a handful of people on the planet who knew the island operation even existed. He dismantled the simple operative hardware of the teleportation booth in the shed, knowing he could construct another such booth anywhere, anytime on short notice. The booth was needed only for the launch, so to speak. The GPS in the jumpsuit took care of the so-called landing area, which could be pre-determined to be anywhere, preferably out of sight of prying eyes.

Just before noontime that day in the seaside Massachusetts town, Alex Bean was walking down Elm Street, alone with his thoughts. He was trying to figure why Manny was present at the bridge the night the island lights did not show, but absent the nights they did.

Was this a big deal? Probably not, Alex tried to convince himself. However, the newspaperman was anxious to speak to Manny, a close acquaintance of the Bean family for years, about it.

Alex shied away from the sometimes public hysteria over UFOs and aliens, government cover-up conspiracies, and other seemingly spooky happenings. "Keep it real" he often told himself. But what would he do if Manny suddenly and totally admitted to some association with a cover-up of matters of science fiction proportions?

"Never happen," he told himself again. To Alex, speaking with Manny about the topic at hand would be like a detective on a murder case eliminating somebody as a suspect through interrogation.

His chance for that discussion arrived as he was about to enter the Village Grind coffee shop at the foot of Smith Neck Harbor bridge to say hello and blow a kiss to his wife, who would be behind the counter ringing up the latest sale. Manny was walking out, carrying a cardboard tray containing a large iced coffee and a king size honey-glazed blueberry donut. That combo was called the Village Grind Deluxe, a staple of the warm weather crowd who descended on Rockland Point. Nobody knew why it was such a big seller. It was, and that's all that mattered.

Alex once tried to figure it out, even asking the yearly visitors about it soon after his wife and close friend Barbara Engle opened the business, but could not get a definitive answer. He lost sleep over it before convincing himself to not sweat the small stuff.

Now he had bigger things to investigate. Namely such matters as Manny's role or non-role in the island lights situation. Alex refused to refer to the matter as a major mystery, to himself or others. He just wanted to talk to Manny about it. And here he was, face to face with his subject, who was exiting the Village Grind coffee shop.

"Manny, my compade," Alex said in an amateurish Portuguese accent to the handyman, who struggled to balance his late-morning munchies. Manny succeeded while letting the heavy glass door close behind him after he made his way out, using the right side of his body to keep it from slamming.

"Hey, yo Alex. Wassup?" Manny replied in a failed attempt at being a cool dude. He looked in vain for a place to put down his coffee and mega-donut, and then motioned with his head to Alex to go to the handyman's work truck in the donut shop parking lot.

The roof of the truck was as good a place as any to set down the goodies temporarily.

"You see the lights last night?" Manny asked, sensing Alex wanted to chat.

"Yes. And I need to speak to you about that."

"Oh. About what, exactly?" Manny was confident any discussion on the current subject would lead nowhere because of his early morning clean-up of the evidence.

"Just wondering, Manny. Why are you never around on the bridge on the nights the lights appear, but there on the nights they don't?"

"Oh, that. You found me out, you little rascal," Manny shot back, affecting a persona of false disappointment. "Why, the truth is I am on a secret mission and I control the island lights and the fog the next morning. Forbes Island is used for the disposal of teleportation tubes, a secret government project."

Confident he had kept the island goings-on hidden in plain sight, he broke into a laugh while pointing at Alex with both hands. "You should have seen the look on your face, Mr. Newspaperman. For a while there I thought you actually believed me. There were a few times I showed up on the bridge when the lights showed, but I got caught up in a conversation with some visitors who spoke Portuguese. I did wave to you and Woody and your wives, but I guess you didn't see me. The lighting on the bridge isn't that bright sometimes."

"OK, I'll buy that. But you have to clear up the fog scenario for me. Why is there always fog the morning after, then you show up at the Village Grind soon after that?"

"That's rich," Manny replied with a chuckle. 'Clear up the fog scenario'. But seriously, Alex, you're not suggesting..."

"Of course not Manny. It's just that this has been in the back of my mind for a while. All I need is for you to look me in the eye and tell me this seeming coincidence is nothing and there is no Twilight Zone or X Files mystery at play here."

"Let me throw this out there," Manny said. "I do a lot of work for Mr. Forbes on his properties around here. Let me take you out to the island in a few days and show you all around. You will see there is nothing there that would support any conspiracy theory."

He knew the evidence was destroyed. Even the cabin and the shed, if they ventured to that part of the island, would appear benign and Manny would casually mention Mr. Forbes used those structures as a getaway - the cabin as a place to relax, and the shed for storage of whatever.

Manny said 'so long' to his friend, put his coffee and donut in the truck cab, buckled up and drove down Bay View Road toward home. His mind raced with the thoughts of the time when his work in Rockland Point would help make the town known to the world.

As he neared his driveway, his mind wandered back to his and his wife's early days in The Group, a quasi-governmental agency that existed to ensure the completion of secret projects. Some of those projects, once completed, could be totally revealed to the public. Other projects would remain secret.

His wife's task in The Group was to provide disinformation to the media whenever members of the public claimed to have witnessed weird happenings, including strange lights or UFO-type craft anywhere in the country.

TENDING TO BUSINESS

Chapter 7

Hamilton's plan to methodically eliminate the Village Grind coffee shop's existence so he could take over the building was in gear. He referred to this segment of the overall plan for Rockland Point as 'The Process.'

He didn't expect The Process to happen overnight while he simply did not know how long it would take. When it did happen, he was sure, the public would consider it to be nothing more than business taking its natural course.

"If there ever was a building in the perfect place," he said to himself, "this is it. That business will close eventually, I will take over the building, and the next step in the plan for Rockland Point will be well on the way to fruition."

He recalled a conversation he had with Manny about a week before.

"I was charged with overseeing the plan," he said to the handyman at the time. "This is a top-secret, quasi-governmental covert project and I am flattered to have been chosen."

"And you should be," Manny said. "There are only a dozen or so hand-picked individuals, who never even heard of Rockland Point until recently, getting this plan off the ground. But we both know the designated work force will be pouring into Rockland Point at some point. That's when the real work will begin."

He told Manny it was the coffee shop building takeover he was now concerned with. It might not be happening, he reminded Manny during that conversation last week, if not for his clandestine establishment of a half dozen or so coffee and donut places named Mega Java near the Deermont-Rockland Point line. They undercut the prices of places such as the harbor-side Village Grind, thus attracting the traffic of those heading to Rockland Point, as well as town residents.

By design, Hamilton's name did not appear on any documents relating to the new businesses at and near the town line.

"That Village Grind's business is declining," Hamilton told himself. "The building's mortgage is becoming more and more difficult for the present owners to pay, and with no hefty capital reserves, or the viable collateral needed to secure a small business loan, the owners Sandra Bean and Barbara Engle will have to go out of business. I'll offer my condolences and quickly purchase the building for a price they can't refuse."

According to plan, he would then convert the building into a boating supply business, giving him the perfect cover to be on the premises, often along with fellow operatives who would supposedly be purchasing boating gear along with unsuspecting locals. After all, the business would be literally a few yards from the harbor where modest pleasure craft, skiffs, yachts and the like were moored when the weather was warm. It would be a perfect front for the next step in what was in the offing for Rockland Point.

In cold New England weather the seasonal population dwindled and ice and freezing, choppy water replaced the seagoing craft in the harbor. The Group's cover plan would then be for the property to be available for storage of half-dozen or so boats while the in-store operation would be open for any local who happened to need anything marine-related.

Hamilton called his sister, Alvaretta, in Washington State on a secure phone line.

"I have to get back to Starling later today," Hamilton said. "Our brother's almost done drawing up the plans for the tunnel system that's going to lead from the basement of the house on Prospect Street to the building I will buy, then to the property behind the art gallery."

There was a prolonged silence at Alvaretta's end of the phone, finally broken by her sniffle. Hamilton knew what was happening. "I know, sis. You wish my wife could be here to see all of this unfolding. I miss her, too. But I don't need to tell you that. She died of cancer way too young. But let's please drop that part of the discussion."

Alvaretta got the message and quickly changed the subject.

"Have you checked the open field on the property in back of the art gallery?" she asked her brother.

"No. It's way too early."

"Agreed, but it won't hurt to send up that drone once in a while to snap off a few pictures so the two families living near there will get used to seeing you operating that remote control pad for the drone. To them, it will seem like some older guy acting like a kid with a new toy."

"Very funny, sister."

Then Hamilton's tone of voice became terse. "Lookit," he said. "There won't be any sense in using the drone before we at least start work on the tunnel system. We don't want to draw any undue attention to the place."

"Understood, Hamilton. If you need anything else in the line of paperwork for the project, let me know."

"Right, sis. Soon I can call in the crew who will pretend to be harbor-side visitors and we can lay the groundwork for putting this town on the evening news, CNN, Fox, Univision, Telemundo, MSNBC, every talk show in existence and, of course, social media."

"But don't get ahead of yourself, Hamilton. You, the master of the occasional cliché, always tell everybody else that a journey of a thousand miles begins with a single step. Take your own advice. Focus on the building takeover by the bridge."

"You're right. And remember. Manny, his wife and I pop into The Village Grind often enough to avert any suspicion about us being involved in any shenanigans."

Before they hung up, Alvaretta reminded Hamilton to call their brother.

Hamilton, leaning back in his office swivel chair, wrote that reminder on a Post-It Note and stuck it to wall behind his computer.

The note, as with all written material connected to any of The Group's sensitive activity, was encrypted, although Hamilton had complained to The Group's hierarchy several times about what he considered a weak code pattern that could be broken by people willing to make the effort. But he didn't make policy, and it was often pointed out to him that nobody had yet broken any code established by The Group.

Hamilton leaned forward in his swivel chair and put his elbows on his computer desk and his head in his hands. He put his disagreements with The Group's hierarchy out of his head. "No sense banging my proverbial head against the proverbial wall," he reasoned.

He picked up his secure line phone and called Maria DeMello.

"Hello Maria. I can always tell it's you picking up the phone because you pick it up part way through the second ring. Manny has his own secure line phone, so he never picks up your phone, and you never pick up his."

"A great security tool, Hamilton. You deserve all the credit for implementing that idea. You calibrated the phones to vibrate for 15 seconds before ringing, so we get the time to reach for the phone and answer on the designated ring. Like you told the boss, a pickup on a different ring signals a security breach."

"Well, Maria, I've got an assignment for you. After the Village Grind goes belly-up and we take over the building, there's gonna be lots of activity in town around the house on Prospect Street and the art gallery. We, as in The Group, need you to put out some cover stories about that."

"OK, Hamilton. I know about what's coming up as the next step in the plan, so when that happens I'll spread the word around town and among some of the local media that the Prospect Street house is undergoing major renovations, from the basement to the attic, per order of an anonymous buyer. Or that some historians want to research the house's connection to the Underground Railroad of the slavery days."

"Hey, good idea, Maria. It helps that one of our own happens to own that house."

"That's great, Hamilton. Now lend me an ear and listen to what doozy of a cover story I have for the property behind the art gallery."

"Go ahead. Shoot."

"Well, the story will go: There's a problem with water seeping into the gallery basement, and it may have something to do with a rising water table. Then we can bring in all the crew we need to supposedly survey, dig, haul in all kinds of material, pour concrete, all the while actually preparing the space under the ground in back of the gallery for our very special visitors."

"Sounds good," Hamilton said. "We must have everything in place for the visitors." Then they both hung up.

They both knew those very special visitors would be part of something awesome.

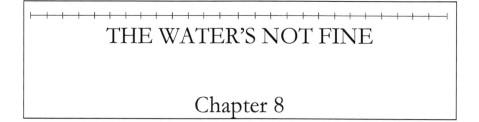

THE WATER'S NOT FINE

Chapter 8

There was a frantic pounding on Alex Bean's front door.

Alex hurriedly dried his dishwashing-wet hands, ran to the door, opened it and saw his pal Woody Engle.

"Woody. What's wrong? Your hair's all wet. I've never seen you look scared like this."

Alex's face quickly switched from a demeanor of concern to one of calm and good humor. "Wait. Is this some rehearsal for one of your roles in a play? Oh, you're good. You are a budding actor with a role coming up in a play with Tom Cruise's cousin. Is this what your role is all about? Hey, c'mon in and dry off."

"This is no joke, Alex."

Woody was shaking like a frightened puppy in a thunderstorm. He strode awkwardly into the living room, accepted a towel from Alex, dried his head and sat in a recliner.

"I was down about 20 feet scuba diving on the land-locked side of the bridge," Woody began between heavy breaths, "and suddenly I felt myself swaying wildly like I was caught in a rip current that kept changing direction. Then I heard a muffled BOOM. I really don't know what came first, it happened so quickly."

Woody hyperventilated, leaned back and stared at the ceiling until his breathing calmed a bit, although his eyes were still somewhat wide and his hands gripped the chair's armrests in the proverbial white-knuckle posture.

"But here's my nightmare, Alex. Right after the swaying and the boom I swear I came face to face with a creature with webbed fingers and a scaly body and head. He had to be at least eight-feet tall. It was like that sea creature on The Twilight Zone episode we watched the other night. I surfaced, bolted out of the water, peeled off my wet suit, kept looking over my shoulder, toweled off as best I could, put on my dry clothes I had in the car. At least I think I did all that. I was in panic mode, and I don't even recall driving here. Sorry I forgot to dry my hair."

Alex cocked his head and gave a smirk that begged the question 'Are you pulling my chain about this sea monster?', and then quickly dismissed that doubt. He was convinced Woody's fear was real, but offered a rational explanation for the underwater encounter.

"You know, Woody, some of those Hollywood folks who summer here could have had something to do with this. Remember last year, I think it was late June, that actor and his fiancée supposedly rehearsed some scenes of their upcoming movie out near where you were scuba diving today. They had some props with them in a boat, put some in the water, and then went on with their rehearsal along with an underwater camera man for the scenes that didn't take place on the yacht."

"Yeah. I remember that day," Woody responded, finally feeling comfortable and secure in his friend's living room. "I remember now. And just like the good citizens of Rockland Point always do, we all just let them go about their business. And we went about ours without gawking in their direction."

"Ahemmmm," Alex intoned, clearing his throat and giving Woody that slightly bowed head, over the glasses 'Excuse me?' look.

"All right, all right," Woody admitted with a red-faced expression of embarrassment. "So I was down at the water's edge that day watching what actors do in rehearsal and taking notes. You know I want to be an actor. I have to learn all I can about the profession. And besides, they've seen me around town. They know I'm not a peeping Tom."

A smile slowly formed on Alex's face. He gave a subtle nod as if that light bulb lit in his mind. "I'll bet my IPhone, golf clubs and stamp collection that the movie they were rehearsing for has something to do with blood thirsty sea creatures in a quiet seaside town. Today you probably came across one of the props from that day last year."

"Wait, my friend," Woody shot back. "Sounds like you're describing the premise of the movie 'Jaws', only not involving a shark."

"I guess we'll just have to wait to find out what's really in that script, won't we?" Alex replied.

But Hamilton Forbes knew exactly what was going on. He happened to be driving by on Water Street when the panic-stricken Woody rocketed out of the harbor waters, yelled to nobody in particular about a "...huge scaly fish man with webbed fingers...", changed up and drove off.

Hamilton, on the verge of becoming livid, called Manny to vent his frustration.

"Manny?" Hamilton said with no hint of good humor in his voice when the Portuguese handyman answered the secure cell phone line.

"What's wrong, Hamilton?"

"Plenty," Hamilton shot back, and then described the statue and its origin. "That statue Lescontis and the contacts managed to send here, ignoring the agreed-upon timeline I might add, apparently sat out in the harbor unbeknownst to anybody until a certain Mr. Woody Engle stumbled across it a few minutes ago. Now we had better pray on our lucky stars there is no follow-up on that."

"Lookit, Hamilton. If there is, I'll just have my wife put out some cover story about pranksters trying to scare local scuba divers, which would have a ring of truth to it. It wouldn't even have to be on the local news - just a story circulating among the townsfolk. You know my wife is good at that sort of thing."

"Of course I do, Manny. That's what she has done for The Group for years. Her cover stories about UFOs, captured aliens and crop circles are works of art. Simple explanations, subtle putdowns and discrediting of eyewitnesses and their accounts to the media along with manufactured exposes of so-called hoaxes. She's so talented in that regard. But she had better be good on this one."

"You got that right," Manny replied, basking in the glow of the compliments to his wife. "I think her gold medal cover story was the one about those chaps in England who, shall we say, confessed to being the culprits behind all those crop circles. Of course they were actors but the mainstream media bought into the ruse and refused to follow up, never asking how the circle makers got from one spot to another in such a short time in so many countries."

"And," Hamilton interjected. "I never saw one interview with any owner of any wheat field where any crop circle appeared. We know The Group had a hand in that."

Manny reminded Hamilton about the previous year's UFO sightings over the vacant field behind the art gallery. Maria planted a story at the time that the bright objects the locals saw were actually sky lanterns launched from an Asian neighborhood in nearby Deermont.

"She nailed that one," Hamilton said. "And of course the compliant mainstream media, even as far away as California and on the network evening news, bought the explanation. How your wife ever got that event and cover story circulated so quickly and so far flung is beyond me. Maria's a genius, Manny."

"And let's not forget," Manny said, "we have an unlikely ally in Alex Bean. He is a skeptical newspaperman, has no clue about what we are doing, and seems to accept so-called logical explanations the mainstream media embraces rather than those put forth by devotees of investigations into UFOs and other strange happenings."

"You are right, Manny. He has covered some of the stories you're talking about, and his take on all of this comes through loud and clear. And he doesn't even know he's helping us keep all of this hidden in plain sight. "

Manny and Hamilton agreed it would be a bad day if Alex started flexing the muscles of his journalistic curiosity and caught on to what Hamilton, Manny, Maria and others from The Group were up to in Rockland Point.

"We have to be sure we don't leave things hanging around, like that statue Woody Engle came across in the harbor, anything related to the teleportation process, Manny."

"I can take a hint, Hamilton. Those tunnels and all that teleportation equipment will be out of sight, or explained away. But it doesn't help that Lescontis jumped the gun by sending that statue without telling anybody."

If Hamilton and Manny knew of Alex's rational explanation to Woody for coming across the scary item in the harbor, they would have thanked him.

Hamilton hung up after saying he would establish a contact with Lescontis and admonish the man for sending the statue without first posting the required message in the field behind the art gallery. He also contacted The Group's recovery team, which would seem to materialize out of thin air whenever objects needed to be taken out of the public eye. Such was the situation with the sea monster statue.

The recovery team's boat was on the scene just minutes after Woody left the area, hauling the statue out of the water and away from prying eyes. Anybody who asked about it would be told the statue was a movie prop which was mistakenly left in the water after a rehearsal. Simple as that.

Hamilton decided he would look at his own actions. He planned to go to the field behind the art gallery and see if he messed up by not looking for the designated sign that would have been placed there to indicate something was being teleported to Rockland Point. Was there a missed encrypted message on his cell phone which would have alerted him to go into action? Lescontis did send the statue, but Hamilton did not know it was coming. Would that jeopardize the entire operation in Rockland Point?

Where exactly was the base of operation for Lescontis?

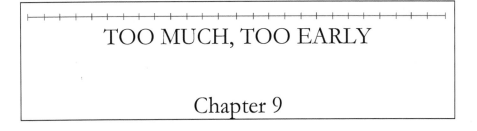

TOO MUCH, TOO EARLY

Chapter 9

Woody was reeling from his face-to-face encounter with what he thought was a horrible sea creature before being calmed down by Alex, and Hamilton was upset with somebody named Lescontis.

As the head operative of The Group's covert mission in Rockland Point, Hamilton needed to get his ducks in a row so the project's cover would not be blown.

Concerned he may have inadvertently missed an alert message from Lescontis concerning the alleged sea creature in the harbor, Hamilton drove out to the art gallery on Russell Road. The lot in back of the gallery was where any alert message was to be placed. He had no idea Lescontis was in the process of contacting him to confess to the mix-up.

With his drone in the back seat, Hamilton purposely parked in the gallery's rear delivery area, in clear view of the two nearby homes.

Rapid-fire thoughts raced through his mind.

How long ago did Lescontis teleport that sea creature statue?...Why didn't he let me know it was coming?...Did he forget Group policy specifically dictates an alert message must always precede the sending of any material?...Did Lescontis's teleportation mechanism malfunction?...I have to send the drone up to click off some photos of the field here to see if he did leave a notification for me....Alvaretta wanted me to send up the drone to get people used to seeing me here with it....I put her off, but now I know she was right....All alert messages are supposed to be at the west end of this lot, and nowhere else.

Hamilton remained seated in his car, reading a newspaper, occasionally glancing out the windshield. He was waiting for some movement, any movement, in any of the yards of the two houses in clear view of the field and the rear of the art gallery. He wanted to be seen with the drone.

After about 10 minutes, a woman stepped out the back door of one of the two nearby homes with her Boston Terrier. The dog sprinted to the backyard chain link fence, propped itself against it and gave a wide-eyed, body wiggling squeal of welcome to Hamilton, who was getting out of his car about 20 feet away.

"Good morning Mr. Forbes," the woman said with a smile and wave. "I see my puppy wants you to come over and play, but he has to go to the vet for a checkup in a few minutes. Then I want to stop by that new Bulgarian gift shop my friends Keith, Kathy and Emma own so I can check it out."

After his own smile and wave of acknowledgment, Hamilton made a deliberate move to take out his drone and send it up, making small talk with the woman all the while. It was crucial she notice his action with the drone, as if he was just some older guy playing with a toy, not involved in an ongoing covert project in Rockland Point.

The small craft went up after Hamilton calibrated the drone's camera and checked the monitor screen on his remote control pad. He would scan the field for any signal from Lescontis.

"He needs to pay attention to what he is told," an irritated Hamilton said under his breath, not caring if anybody saw him talking to himself, although nobody outside of a foot or two from him could hear him. "He knows. Lescontis knows. We have a timeline for Rockland Point's reveal to the world and he needs to follow it."

The drone clicked off dozens of pictures, none showing the alert message Lescontis would have been expected to have sent.

The drone was retrieved and put in the back seat of the car. Hamilton whipped out his cell phone. Leaning against the car, he took a deep breath, told himself to relax and calm down, and successfully did so.

He listened to the phone ringing at the other end as he held the phone to his right ear with one hand and opened the driver's side door with the other. He made sure the car windows were closed as he slid onto the seat. He started the engine and was confident nobody could overhear his conversation. Manny answered the secure line.

"Hamilton, what's cookin'"?

"Lescontis is going to blow this whole operation," Hamilton responded, now calm and speaking in a measured manner. "He's their Manny, but he has to realize this operation can't succeed unless we all do our assigned tasks in the proper order."

"You are too kind," Manny said. "You say he is the 'Manny' at that end of the operation. He does there and then basically what I'm doing here and now with the travel."

"Well," Hamilton replied, "I have no problem comparing him to you, rather than you to him, if you know what I'm saying. In any event, I don't want to get sidetracked. I called to tell you something must be done, and soon.

"We both know Lescontis sent the sea creature statue well before he was supposed to, and without coordinating with anybody. Therefore I never got a coded phone message from The Group, so I had no way of knowing to look for it because it was unauthorized in our project timeline. If there is something you can do to block any unauthorized transmittals of material, please do."

"Let me work on it," Manny said. "In the meantime, in case there are any questions by locals about that statue being retrieved, my wife will circulate a story about some actors having accidentally left it there after rehearsing a movie scene."

"That's genius, Manny. The movie types around here are always rehearsing scenes or checking out places to do script run-throughs. I love hiding things in plain sight."

Hamilton then returned to the scenario at hand.

"I guess it turns out Lescontis started feeling his oats," he said. "I don't like it one bit, not one iota. That statue was supposed to come here later and be used as proof of what this covert project is all about. Now that Mr. Engle has seen it and will be spreading the word about having seen it, it is useless for the intended purpose. I'll bring it out to the art gallery and put it on display. We'll put a plaque with it saying it was done by some 'budding sculptor' in the area who wishes to remain anonymous."

"But Hamilton, what will we say is the reason it was found underwater?"

"Like I said. We'll say the so-called budding sculptor sold it to some movie company to use as a prop for a scene rehearsal. That cannot be denied by anybody since it never happened and there's nobody to check with."

Hamilton assured Manny word would get back to Lescontis the statue arrived, that he has to do what he is told, when he is told, adding "We can't screw up this project. There has been too much effort, too many people and much too much planning put into it."

"I hear you," Manny said. "If people around here figure out what's happening right under their noses, this project will fall flat. There would be too much interference from those outside the loop who would want to profit from all The Group's planning and hard work."

"No kidding," Hamilton answered. "If we even suspect someone around here has figured out what's going on, we'll have to do everything in our power to silence them."

Manny heard the words 'silence them' from time to time, always knowing the sinister-sounding phrase meant simply putting some disinformation story or stories out there for public consumption.

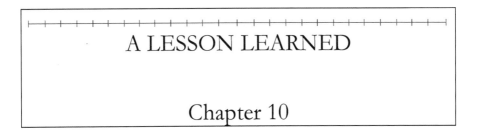

A LESSON LEARNED

Chapter 10

Lescontis reached with his thumb and forefinger for the pull knob on the small door to the message cubicle on the edge of his wooden table. Still seated after his morning meal, he opened the cubicle, which was only big enough to accommodate his hand and maybe a slip of paper.

The incessant, annoying clicking of a crude metronome had alerted him to the arrival of the message on the piece of paper now in his hand. The clicking stopped and the slightly pungent odor and misty vapors dissipated.

Lescontis, talking in a language known only to his island community, spoke to his wife, Sancar.

"I have been chided in writing from those not so much far from us in distance but well forward from us in time," he told her. "I accidently sent the sea creature monument to that land afar sooner than I had been instructed."

"We must obey the people there," Sancar said in the language while sweeping bread crumbs away from Lescontis's table with the help of the hem of her toga. "Did you enjoy your morsels from the cooking box?" she asked as an aside.

He answered, "Yes. Those waves of mystical workings I was directed to pursue make that box a treasure for our people. I am much heartened to have been contacted by those in the land thousands of years ahead of us. They were doing near magical attempts to talk to us while we were likewise seeking to speak with humans in another land and not near us in time. They imparted knowledge to me, which I have been able to direct into such things as the cooking box.

"I must quickly set myself to be not so excited with the large closet box which once contained the sea creature statue to send to those faraway people so I do not err in this way again. My curious attention to it caused me to touch the sending buttons accidentally which caused it to travel to them wrongly and certainly without notification. Our marvelous new-found knowledge makes a galaxy of time small enough to put in a toga pocket. Both our peoples have been on this heavenly body they call earth for thousands of seasons. They first believed we reside in a land called Atlantis, which we know of only from glorious, fanciful stories."

The island where Lescontis and Sancar did reside would not be found on any map in Rockland Point or the largest library anywhere in the world. It no longer exists. Its connection to Rockland Point was born of that coincidence of scientific discovery by advanced minds both in The Group and on the island of Lescontis and his peers.

Time travel scientists working in harmony with The Group had been attempting for years to reach anybody in a distant time. By coincidence, advanced wise thinkers on the island of Lescontis and Sancar were doing likewise. In one magical moment both attempts slammed into each other, alerting both sides to the sweet realization of success.

The two would-be time travel ventures began a communication which might never be known to the world.

"Shame it is that all the people from afar know not the true meaning of the sea creature statue," Sancar said. "They may have thought it by itself to be not a good representation. But we are well happy with it because it is really meant to be placed in our living time side-by-side with a well-liked angel image of a larger size."

"Yes, Sancar. Our expression of good towering over evil. I wish I had not made the error of sending one statue without the other. That would not have happened had I adhered to the appointed moment to send them both."

"It may be just as well, Lescontis. While those far away may fret over the confusion of suddenly seeing the statue, it will distance their curiosities from the real purpose of what they are seeing."

"Ahhh, Sancar. These are the moments we have arranged with those from afar. We and those in the league called The Group will be in control as we do the bidding only we know of at this time."

She smiled and placed her hand on her seated husband's shoulder. "Let us not forget and let us convey to The Group our concern for the result of what is being put into action."

"You are right, Sancar. If our and The Group's plan is discovered before it is ready to be placed into the lives of those so far hence, it will be forever ruined. All the power we would have had over them will be spirited into the possession of the wrong people. Those who would do conceit and selfish ventures."

Sancar nodded.

They embraced; confident this plan would be put into action with the desired result.

Sancar smiled with pride, remembering what her husband said to her months ago.

"We must repay them," he had said at the time. "They imparted to us knowledge to construct items we may use each day, such as the cooking box, to better our conveniences. Now we will be in concert with The Group to repay them in that place of the name Rockland Point."

MAKING THE CONNECTION

Chapter 11

Lescontis leaned back in his chair, hands clasped behind his head. He closed his eyes but did not doze off. His thoughts drifted to that day about two years before when he was seated with his four colleagues at the island's science council chambers. The five comprised the island's Conclave of Wisdom, whose counterpart was The Group.

The conclave leader, Imparo, reminded Lescontis and the others at the time in the language known only to the islanders, "The five of us here and our workers of science must keep today's achievement to ourselves for the moment to avoid our populace thinking we are a group of mentally mad wise thinkers."

Lescontis asked Imparo to state the achievement.

"The effort and time we have used to establish a method to speak with other humans far distant from us in time has met a curious and most likeable circumstance," Imparo said. "Doing our usage this morning of the implements we have constructed, with metal and magnetic pieces, we have received signals."

"What are these signals of which you speak, Imparo?"Lescontis wanted to know. "Our knowledge and ability to make devices such as you speak of are very limited. But to have accomplished a success of such high excellence is quite heartening. Are we to seriously believe your report?"

"Yes, it is to be believed. The signals are from peoples we discovered were attempting to communicate with anybody far distant in time, either in their past or their future in a manner in which we were attempting to reach any time-distant peoples."

Another council member, with knowledge of the discovery by the workers of science, joined the conversation.

"The signals were acknowledged, knowing we had much concern about our differences in language. Using pleasant-sounding tones like that of music, we conveyed our pleasure in contacting them. They responded at the same level of pleasantness, and neither of us needed to speak words."

As all five council members knew very soon, Lescontis recalled wise minds from both parties departed from musical tones and assumed a manner of communication of devised words, including encrypted messages, which facilitated contact between the island's Conclave of Wisdom and The Group. It was not long before the conclave received instructions on the building of the time travel mechanism which prematurely carried the statue to the harbor in Rockland Point.

His recollection of that day with the conclave ended as he sat up straight at the sound of Sancar's voice.

"Here is the tablet of methods of encryption you asked of so your words to those in the land of Rockland Point are not misunderstood," she said. Sancar was not a member of the conclave, but she held a position of trust with the island's scientific community. She circulated stories among her land's populace which would deflect attention from the secretive actions of the Conclave of Wisdom in sending material and messages to Rockland Point. Sancar was to the Conclave what Manny's wife, Maria, was to The Group.

"I must relay to them my desire to know what other materials they wish me to transport to them and when," Lescontis said. "I will be serious to notify the man of the name Hamilton that I will be sure to follow his direction of placing proper notification in a timely way from this time forward. I will also emit gratitude to a person they indentify as Manny for providing knowledge to us about construction of items which allow us to send materials through time."

But could Rockland Point, and the rest of the world, be expected to express gratitude for what the Conclave would someday teleport to them?

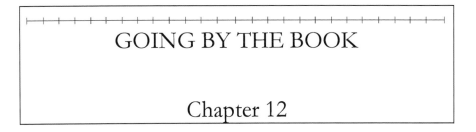

GOING BY THE BOOK

Chapter 12

The assembly hall in the basement of the First Congregational Church of Rockland Point was buzzing with chatter from 100 or so people on a warm Wednesday evening.

The white clapboard house of worship on Center Street was the gathering place for Sunday services, Cub Scout and Boy Scout and Girl Scout weekly meetings, a women's group known as "The Sewing Circle", support groups of various descriptions and an after-school program for kids whose parents both worked.

The church's message board on the manicured front lawn announced the reason for this day's occupants: "Rockland Point Honors the Persons of the Year - Manny and Maria DeMello"

The DeMellos, observing etiquette and arriving fashionably late as guests of honor, walked from the parking lot toward the assembly hall's side door as directed.

They paused to take in their fame on the message board.

"Manny, it is days like this that make us proud to be Portuguese. Our whaling ancestors picked a beautiful spot to settle and raise families. And I am so fortunate to have been born and raised here where we met and married. After, of course, we did some traveling around the country as directed by The Group."

This evening's festivities, Manny figured, would be just as good a time as any to talk to Hamilton about what was next in the covert project in Rockland Point. Hamilton, as last year's person of the year, would be at the head table along with the DeMellos.

"Hamilton and I can just chat away," Manny told Maria, "and if anybody happens by while we are in the midst of some sensitive discussion, either Hamilton or I will simply say something like, '...in this book I am reading.' and no one will be the wiser. That's how we can silence people. I can be as detailed as I want about the plans for Rockland Point, and eavesdroppers will be convinced it is all science fiction in some book."

Maria quizzed him, "But what if the person hearing what you are saying becomes interested and wants to know where he or she can buy that book?"

"OK. What if I tell them...oops. Let's cut the talk for now." Manny directed Maria's attention to a distant figure.

It was Alex Bean, a good 20 or 30 yards away, poking his head out of the assembly hall's side door.

"Time for your grand entrance," the newspaper man, who just alerted the crowd inside, called to the couple.

After a moment or two to take a few deep breaths and prepare for any emotions that might crop up, the DeMellos locked arms, grew broad smiles and strode down the four steps into the assembly hall to a standing ovation. A massive banner in back of the room declared 'Welcome Persons of the Year'.

Alex and his wife, Sandra, along with the Beans' close friends Woody and Barbara Engle, the four of whom organized the evening's event, applauded from the head table. Woody then slipped away pretty much undetected.

It was not easy for Sandra and Barbara to bask in the evening's festive atmosphere. The Village Grind coffee and donut shop they owned was going up for sale the next day. The business's financial picture had become just too bleak.

Manny and Maria made their way to the head table, acknowledging well wishes and congratulations along the way. They shook hands with those near them at the seats of honor, and then slid into their chairs as the applause subsided.

"Welcome to our couple of the year," master of ceremonies Alex declared. "Manny and Maria, you have earned this honor through your work in this community. Manny, with your abilities and work ethic that has made this a truly beautiful place. The landscaping you maintain free of charge on the grounds of our town hall on Dartmouth Street is priceless. That's why it was featured in 'Lawns and Grounds' magazine last month.

"And Maria," Alex continued with a subtle hand gesture in her direction. "Well, what can I say that the townsfolk don't already know?" The audience nodded and smiled.

"You pride yourself in volunteering at the local food pantry, the hospital and Rides for Seniors, which, as we all are aware, provides transportation for the elderly to doctor appointments, pharmacies and food shopping. And I can say without fear of contradiction...I must apologize for the cliché but it is true...I can say there are several in attendance tonight, including our wonderful Portuguese community, whose lives have been touched in some way by your unselfish devotion to the health and welfare of our citizens."

The audience applauded again but remained seated as the evening's guests of honor stood with self-conscious smiles and nods.

"On with the show," Alex said loudly and with a broad smile, pointing with both hands to a door slowly opening from a room at the side of the assembly hall.

The audience went suddenly silent, and then erupted in laughter as Woody emerged from behind the open door sporting a long-hair wig, rouge colored cheeks and an apron. He was impersonating Maria. This was in Woody's zone of comfort as he loved the craft of acting and had dreams of making a living on stage and screen.

Woody strode to the front of the head table, looked at Maria and batted his eyes. She smiled. Woody turned to face the gathering and attempted to affect a female voice.

"I don't have time to finish all my baking today," Woody said while slapping his hands to the side of his face. "I have so much to do. I need gas in my car to drive Mr. Hackmire to a doctor appointment. Then there's the grocery store run for half the people on Bridge Street, and I'm committed to four hours at the food pantry."

After another three or four minutes imitating one half of the honored couple, Woody abruptly took off his wig and untied the apron, placing it on the head table.

With a serious expression, he panned the hushed crowd, took a deep breath and spoke in his normal voice, wavering slightly with emotion.

"Mrs. DeMello is a good sport and we had a few laughs at her expense. But make no mistake; there is nothing light-hearted about who she is and what she does for people. A well-deserved honor today for her." Woody turned to Maria and gave her a big smile as the gathering stood and clapped.

Woody gave a slight wave and a wink to the crowd and walked back into the room from which he had emerged a few minutes before. The audience suspected something and chuckled in anticipation.

Then it happened. Woody, with an oversized fake handlebar moustache and wearing a tool belt that was over laden with every handyman tool imaginable and drooping almost to his knees, loped his way to the table of honor again.

Manny flung his head back, laughing heartily and clapping in earnest. He then spoke to Woody in jest, "You look more like that Mario in the video game than me. Hey, you forgot the cement trowel in the tool belt. Remember I used it last summer when I put in the walkway from your patio to the driveway?"

"Touché," Woody responded before continuing his handyman act. It included some one-liners and comic pantomime of Manny clipping a hedge. The latter was a big hit with the gathering as Woody clipped the imaginary hedge with imaginary clippers, stepped back to assess his work, clipped, stepped back, clipped, stepped back, over and over again, never satisfied.

Then off came the costume, the moustache needing an extra tug to escape the adhesive, as Woody became serious.

"One more time," Woody said. "Manny and Maria do not take themselves too seriously, as we have seen. But we do take them seriously when it comes to making our community the best it can be. The Person of the Year committee considered many factors in making this year's selection. These included character, participation in community affairs, contributions to the welfare of others among other things."

After the event's New England style clam boil dinner featuring seafood chowder, lobster and corn on the cob followed by homemade apple pie, attendees stood one at a time and praised and thanked the DeMellos, sometimes tearfully and sometimes in Portuguese.

Alex then announced a 15-minute break before an official presentation ceremony.

Manny got Hamilton's attention a couple of chairs down at the head table then nodded and silently mouthed the words "Let's meet outside."

They found a spot near a large tree in back of the church, peered left and right and were satisfied they were out of earshot of all others.

"Tomorrow I'll start work on the passage way from the basement of the house on Prospect Street to the water," Manny told Hamilton. "I should have the teleportation booth on Forbes Island soon."

"While you're doing that," Hamilton said, "I'll start shipping in the workers who will be housed in the barracks under the lot behind the art gallery. And like we planned, any prying eyes there wondering about all the digging and concrete pouring will be placated by the simple explanation of a troublesome rising water table and relocation of subterranean pipes. That should silence the curious."

The underground barracks and all its proposed functions required 40-50 individuals for the labor and scientific end of The Group's Rockland Point project.

Hamilton spotted two couples sauntering near the tree and began the diversion tactic - audibly.

"You know, Manny, in this science fiction book I'm reading, about 50 people were sent to a secret location behind an art gallery. They were working on an underground bunker where a crew was getting ready for one of the biggest reveals in the history of mankind."

"I think I read that book, too," Manny said, with the two couples still within earshot. "The materials they were going to use, like desks, beds and laboratory equipment were going to be there ahead of time. The small items would be brought through a tunnel system to the underground area."

"And you know what?"Hamilton added. "I think I remember the story saying there was some venue about halfway through the tunnel system to verify what was sent from the basement of the house was what was on the way to the barracks."

That halfway venue was soon to be in possession of The Group. The harbor-side building which housed the Village Grind was about to go up for sale and Hamilton would buy it from Sandra and Barbara.

"Hey, it's time to go back inside, Manny. Things are about to wrap up."

The evening's event concluded with a formal presentation of the award for Manny and Maria. It was announced their names would be added to the town's Wall of Honor in front of the town hall. This night's honorees spoke briefly in appreciation of the award.

Then everybody headed home. Hamilton had a big day ahead of him. He was going to buy some property and let The Group know it would not be long before Rockland Point became world famous.

AN OFFER THEY COULDN'T REFUSE

Chapter 13

The Village Grind had its "Building 4 Sale" sign in the front window for about an hour following its usual 7 a.m. opening time. It was the morning after the town's annual Person of the Year festivities. Some people heading onto the Smith Neck Harbor Bridge gave the sign a curious side glance, while others popped inside to satisfy their curiosity and offer sincere, and sometimes obligatory, condolences to co-owners Sandra Bean and Barbara Engle.

One of those who popped in was Hamilton.

"I am so sorry this business didn't work out for you," he said to the both of them, who were wiping down the counter to stay busy through the dearth of customers.

"Thank you so much," Sandra said. "Barbara and I gave it a go, but business dropped off quite suddenly over the past year, and we couldn't figure out why, except maybe for the Mega Java coffee and donut places on the outskirts of town. They undersold us, and being novices in the business world, we did not know how to compete."

Hamilton fought diligently and successfully to suppress a guilty visage.

"Well," he said. "You probably still have a mortgage on this place, and I would like to make you an offer for the building. This would be a perfect spot for me to open a marine supply and repair business, being adjacent to the moorings in the harbor and all."

"We're doing this as a 'for sale by owner' transaction," Sandra replied as a negotiation tactic, "and need to recoup so many expenses like those mortgage payments, taxes, inventory contracts with the bakery supply people in Deermont and whatever bills go along with maintaining a business."

The millionaire took out a notepad, smiled at the duo, ripped out a blank page and scribbled a dollar figure on it. He handed it to Barbara, who showed it to Sandra. They each grew a smile.

"You wouldn't be toying with us, Mr. Forbes, would you? Barbara and I don't need any jokesters at this point. This transaction is born out of necessity, not pleasure."

"No. This figure, which I realize may look like more than enough, is a legitimate offer. I definitely want this property. And having known the Bean and Engle families for all these years, I feel comfortable making this offer. After all - and I do not mean any conceit in saying this - I can afford it."

The trio made arrangements to meet at the office of attorney Wesley Plugman the following day to complete the transaction. The lawyer was a family friend to both parties.

Sandra hung the "closed" sign on the donut shop's glass front door and the two soon-to-be erstwhile business owners hopped into Barbara's car to go hang out, and possibly shed a few tears, at the Bean house.

"Well, here's what Hamilton wrote as a dollar figure, and he signed it," Sandra said, holding the piece of paper she planned to show Alex when he and Woody returned from a venture about 20 miles out of town. Alex had an assignment from the Deermont Times to do a story on the Bridgeriver Triangle. He was bringing Woody along for company.

"I hope our husbands are having a good time at the Triangle," Barbara said, hopefully changing the subject from the conclusion of their once-joyful attempt at running a business. "I don't put much stock in all the legends and so-called mysterious sightings there. It's always called America's Bermuda Triangle, but it's entirely on land, except for a few ponds here and there. It reminds me a lot of those theories of the origin of those lights over Forbes Island."

"I know," Sandra said. "Alex doesn't buy into the Bridgeriver Triangle mystery, either. But his paper wants him to do a story about it. They do one every few years. Sort of a way to keep the legend alive and maybe lure tourists to the area. Maybe his editor thought a skeptic's perspective might be a fresh approach."

The Bridgeriver Triangle, when viewed on a map, did have three fairly distinct points of land which suggested a noticeable shape and hence its name. Its area included four or five small towns and was no more than 15 miles from Rockland Point.

Barbara told Sandra of a recollection of her Uncle Richard's tale of strange happenings one day at that area of mystery.

"He said he was just out for a walk on a brisk fall Saturday in a wooded area of one of the towns in the triangle, I don't remember which town. But he said he was stopped on a path to the woods by a soldier holding a rifle and told sternly to leave the area. Uncle Ricky, as we called him, said he first thought there were some National Guard maneuvers going on in the woods. No big deal, so he left and drove back home."

"I give up," Sandra responded. "What - happened - next?"

"Well, as he drove down Cadbunker road toward home, he said he heard a loud crackle followed by a very short but very loud hum, then his car was encased by a dense fog, which cleared up in just a few seconds. Then he said he heard what sounded like a helicopter. He looked into his rearview mirror and didn't see any aircraft rising or descending."

"What did he find out?"

"Nothing. He said he asked a co-worker at Deermont Machine Tooling, who was a National Guard colonel, about it. The guy said he knew nothing about what Uncle Ricky was talking about, sort of laughing it off. So my uncle chalked it up to just another tale of the Bridgeriver Triangle, maybe figuring some sort of military routine training, like helicopter landings and takeoffs, but nothing earth-shaking, took place."

"He was probably right, Barbara. Like Alex told me once, 'If we knew the truth to some of life's mysteries, we'd probably be so bored we would wish we never asked about it in the first place.' "

"But," Barbara chimed in, "don't forget. The name Bridgeriver Triangle did have a somewhat charming origin. Supposedly the early settlers in this part of Massachusetts learned about it from the local Native Americans. The Indians considered the triangle's land to be similar to a bridge over some river of mystery. There is no record of the Indian name for it, so through the centuries, the name became Bridgeriver Triangle."

Barbara recalled a recent article in 'Bay State Pathways' magazine. "That's where I read that the word triangle was added after some centuries-ago cartographer indicated that configuration on a map."

Sandra glanced at Barbara, smiled and offered, "Maybe there were unexplainable, at least in the 1600s and 1700s, sightings and happenings in the Bridgeriver Triangle. Like the lights over Forbes Island? You think? Or maybe it was a portal for time travel. Sorry 'bout that. My imagination got me a little carried away."

In unison, the two women attempted some eerie-sounding ghost noises, and then laughed before Barbara interjected a sobering thought.

"We don't have an explanation for everything that's happening in our world, do we?"

Their car pulled into the Beans' driveway and parked next to Alex's.

"Now that the two adventurers are back home, we can show them the unofficial bill of sale from Hamilton." Sandra said. "They knew we were posting the 'For Sale' sign at the shop today, but they'll likely be as shocked as we were at the size of the offer and how quickly it came."

Sandra opened the front door to her house to find Woody and Alex sitting in the living room watching ESPN.

Without taking his eyes off the TV, Alex blurted out, "Welcome home ladies. My, you're early." He then sensed something was up and turned to face the women. "Hey, aren't you supposed to be putting in full days at the shop until it sells, whenever that may be, like in several weeks or so, or maybe months? Why did you close up so early today? Is everything OK?"

Sandra held the makeshift bill of sale as if reading it.

"Well, gentlemen, Barbara and I have good news and bad news."

Woody, sitting in a chair next to Alex, touched his friend's arm and declared to him in an aristocratic tone, "Allow me."

Looking at the wives, he said, "OK, I'll bite. Give us the bad news first."

"It all has to do with the piece of paper Sandra's holding." Barbara began. "We no longer, as of tomorrow morning, have a donut shop. The place we put so much work into, the business we once wanted so badly. It's gone, finito, ain't no more, a piece of history."

"You don't seem too upset," Alex replied with an inquisitive look.

"Well," Sandra said, getting to her good news. "Hamilton made an offer on the donut shop building less than an hour ago, and he's paying cash. We couldn't turn it down. It covers all our business debt, the mortgage, all the odds and ends we owe on, plus some left over. Here Alex, here's the slip of paper with his offer and he signed it."

"Let me see that paper." Alex went silent, furrowed his brow. "Wow. I mean double wow. Woody, you have to see this."

Woody saw, and then wanted to know something. "Is the decimal point in the right place? Is this some sort of sick joke on Hamilton's part?"

Sandra and Barbara assured him and Alex it was not, noting it would all be an officially-done deal, aside from some routine paperwork, after the visit to the lawyer's office the following morning.

SIGNED, SEALED, DELIVERED…NOW WHAT?

Chapter 14

The session at attorney Plugman's office with Hamilton, Barbara and Sandra was routine in the eyes of the lawyer, but Hamilton was aware of the world-wide implications of the purchase of the now-former donut shop.

"I need the two of you to just sign here," attorney Plugman said as he slid a paper across a dark oak table to Sandra and Barbara, who were sitting next to Hamilton.

They did as instructed, and then slid the paper over to Hamilton.

He signed, leaned over the table and shook hands with the lawyer before looking over to the two now-former business owners.

"I know things didn't quit turn out they way you young ladies planned when you opened the Village Grind. But I am well aware of the sense of perseverance in both your families. There is no doubt in my mind you will survive this disappointment and maybe enter into another business venture somewhere down the road."

Barbara spoke first.

"Well, that's very nice of you to show that confidence in us, Mr. Forbes. Thank you. Yes, this business failure was a disappointment, but you were extremely generous to us and that means we have no worries about paying off our business debts and having some left over."

Then Sandra chimed in.

"I'm not sure all this has sunk in yet. I might even cry my eyes out when I get home. Opening that donut shop was a dream event for Barbara and me. Now the dream is over. However, Mr. Forbes, you are a very compassionate human being. You and I can agree money can't always buy happiness, although what you have done for us does ease the pain a bit."

The parties in the signing bid each other 'Have a nice day' and went their separate ways - Sandra and Barbara to the Beans' house, attorney Plugman to his private office, and Hamilton to his car for the 15-minute drive to his house to meet Manny, who was waiting for him in the driveway.

"Well, the donut shop building is now ours," Hamilton said to his Group colleague as they entered the house. "You can finish up that tunnel from the shore near the Cluff house to the building we just bought. Then finish the tunnel route to the art gallery."

"Sounds good, Hamilton. Hey, and before I forget, we still have to deal with the Bridgeriver Triangle situation. It no longer fits into our plans for Rockland Point, but people may continue to talk about it and start poking their noses of curiosity into things better left hidden in plain sight. And even though the Triangle is not now in the plan for Rockland Point, it might come into play later on for matters relating to other projects. That's why we were instructed to pretty much leave things alone there."

Hamilton gave Manny a nod of understanding, then added: "Even with the legend of this Triangle business, the lights similar to those over the island, strange noises, and Indian folklore of spirits appearing and then disappearing, odd-looking aircraft supposedly landing and taking off. Then there's anecdotal evidence of government intervention - military personnel turning people away from innocent walks in the woods around the triangle. All this activity."

"No need to worry, my millionaire friend. My wife will continue to take care of all the suspicions. Maria always comes up with cover stories that debunk the stories of things like aliens from outer space and discredit anybody who suggests there are other-worldly events taking place here. The time-travel, the upcoming miracle in Rockland Point, the contact with the ancient island of Lescontis - all those things are well-hidden from the general public."

But will the Bridgeriver Triangle legend be that easy to explain away?

Hamilton sensed something, gave a look of concern at his friend and spoke with compassion and a sliver of humor.

"Something is bugging you, I can tell. Is it some handyman project you're concerned about? Did the Portuguese national soccer team lose again?"

"No, please Hamilton. This is dead serious. Does everybody know the implications of what is going to happen in Rockland Point? It's going to be a 'feel good' moment, but then what? You know the saying: Be careful what you wish for."

One thing the two always agreed upon in relation to the supposed mysterious happenings in and around Rockland Point was this: Let the skeptics and other-worldly theorists have the first say. Then Maria, under the auspices of The Group, can debunk it all and the Rockland Point project can proceed as planned.

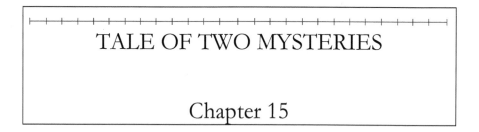

TALE OF TWO MYSTERIES

Chapter 15

Arthur Edwards and Emma Clermont sat behind the anchor desk at Rockland Point's TV channel 12, gently shuffling papers and having their microphones put in place and adjusted by stage staff. It was less than a minute to their noon airtime of the twice-monthly local talk show 'Taking You There.'

The red light on camera one went on and Emma, in her station-issued light blue blazer bearing the channel 12 egg-shaped logo, took the cue.

"Greetings friends, our faithful viewers of WRPD. Today on 'Taking You There', we will take you to the nearby Bridgeriver Triangle, that mysterious section of our county where weird things, identified by some as other-worldly, seem to happen. We will take you there via a discussion with a studio guest."

"That's right, Emma," co-host Arthur, wearing an open collar white shirt under the station blazer, said into camera two. "We are fortunate to have as our guest here in the studio to talk about the Triangle's legendary reputation, Mr. William G. Roberts. He grew up in Colorado, moved here about 10 years ago, and is now professor of philosophy at nearby Deermont Community College. He has written a book."

Arthur held that book up to the camera. The title was 'Two Mysteries to Ponder: The Bridgeriver Triangle and Time Travel in the Old West'.

Wearing wire-rimmed spectacles, the guest looked like a college professor from a 1970s movie in his off-red turtleneck under a grey tweed sport jacket that had oval suede patches on the elbows. Seated next to the co-hosts, he began to speak, but the button microphone in his lapel hummed and let out an annoying screech, making his words inaudible.

He looked into camera one, gave a self-conscious smile and furrowed his brow in an attitude of apology to the viewing audience, while a stage hand fixed the problem.

"I guess those aliens at the Bridgeriver Triangle did some time travel and are now in your control room," professor Roberts said, evoking spontaneous chuckles from Emma and Arthur.

Emma took the lead on the interview.

"Hey. Great segue, professor. You have been outspoken over the years about the Bridgeriver Triangle, saying you believe the supposed strange goings-on there cannot be explained away so easily. We know there have been thousands of reports of odd happenings at the Triangle. Some people have reported seeing alien spacecraft, others have told stories of loud bangs in the woods, pulsating balls of light, images of humans appearing and disappearing, even reports of military personnel approaching joggers on public paths there and ordering them to leave the area."

"You know, Emma...," the professor began, then interjected, "By the way, thank you and Arthur for inviting me here today to talk about my book...," then continued, "You know, I spoke with one citizen who said she was taking an innocent walk in the Triangle woods recently and was shooed away by a military type, and she relayed a fact that I found interesting."

"And that would be?" Arthur asked.

"Well, she said this supposed military guy was dressed oddly. She told me he had on what appeared to be wrinkled and faded Vietnam-era Army fatigues, not the camo type we see nowadays, a helmet liner that did not fit properly - it was too big - and he had no insignias of any kind on the fatigues. She said her gut reaction was that he wasn't official military, but was legit."

"Did she leave?" Emma asked.

"Definitely she did. She didn't suspect anything suspicious at the time by the guy's appearance, figuring, I guess, that it is what it is. She only believed at the time that there was some military exercise going on. The guy was carrying a rifle, but it was strapped over his shoulder, not in a threatening position. She also said he was firm but polite. He called her 'Ma'am' and asked her, not told her, to leave the area."

"I know," Emma said, "you mentioned to our producer yesterday in preparation for this show that this woman thought nothing sinister of the encounter, and simply left the area since the man was courteous."

"That's what I said, Emma. She didn't want to stand in the way of military exercises. There was a story in the Deermont Times a year or so ago about weekend training sessions for Army units from Fort Bristol, not at all combat-related, and people should not worry about it because they just train on things like finding their way out of the woods when lost, things like that."

"And I guess," Arthur chimed in, "they also would appreciate it if the public in general would stay away during those sessions."

"You got it," the professor said. "But this woman, who knows I have a fascination with the Bridgeriver Triangle's legend, contacted me the other day and said she couldn't get that encounter with the military type out of her head. I told her that if somebody was attempting to hide something going on at the Triangle, sending out an intentionally ill-dressed military type would direct the focus to him, away from any covert activity."

"This is starting to read like a mystery novel. Let's hear the next chapter," Arthur chimed in.

"Well, here's the kicker," the professor said, sliding his chair a foot or so closer to the hosts' anchor desk. "She told me that several days before the encounter with G.I. Joe - that's what she called him - she took some pictures of squirrels during her walk in the Triangle woods. In the background of the first photos she took were two massive tree stumps and a distinctive boulder, shaped roughly like a child's booster seat, about three or four feet high."

The professor gently shook an index finger in a demeanor of telling one to pay close attention.

"Then, she returned a day or two later for a walk along the exact same route and saw some squirrels again in the same spot as the first pictures she took and then took some more photos. When she looked at the second set of pictures back home, she was shocked."

"The reason being?" Arthur asked.

"The reason is this. One of the massive tree trunks was tipped over and moved a good four feet to the left. The boulder, that had to weigh at least a ton, maybe more, was turned like 45 degrees. All that movement for no apparent reason."

"I'm curious, professor," Emma said. "Could you at some point get the woman's permission and return to a later show to share the photos with the viewing audience?

"I definitely will contact her, promise. But there was something else this woman noticed. She told me there was some strange, almost putrid, odor around the stumps and boulder. I pressed her to describe it, and she likened the odor to the remnants of an electrical fire."

Arthur looked square into camera one and introduced a station break. "Don't touch that remote. We will be back with our guest after these messages."

The screen showed the cover of the professor's book, which depicted two images: One a forested area shrouded by an aura of yellow and pink, and the other a man in buckskin frontier garb ascending the steps of a neatly-appointed two-story house that appeared contemporary to the 1990s. The book's cover faded to black as the station audio played the theme music from 'The X-Files'.

Back from commercial, Emma gave a brief re-introduction of Professor Roberts, beginning with the obligatory "In case you just joined us..."

Camera two shifted to the professor, who restated his belief in time travel.

"As I stated in my book, although there are naysayers out there who say I should just shut up and get a life, I do believe time travel is scientifically possible. I also mention in my book incidents of time travel involving our military as far back as World War I."

"Yes, I have heard stories like that," Arthur said."

"Exactly, Arthur. But predictably, the government denies any such events ever took place. In my book I present the theory, backed up with verifiable facts, that time travel has taken place. There is a passage in my book about a young girl in the 1940s finding the diary of one of her ancestors, a great-great-grandfather or something whose name was Ebeneezer Corstair, among family papers in her attic. In the diary, according to a story the young girl told to her local newspaper, was an entry about Ebeneezer traveling in the Midwest by covered wagon in the 1800s. In that entry, Corstair says he got lost in a dust storm and took shelter in a nearby dwelling that he described as, well, let me read the passage, listed as March 20, 1846, to you and the viewing audience."

The professor then stated "Here's the diary entry as published in that newspaper article", opened a copy of his book and read:

"The dwelling was something like a palace," Corstair's passage began, "since I have never seen outside porches with such ornate appointments. I could see no signs of life inside the house, so finding an unsecured door with a metal handle in appearance like I had never seen; I entered only for the purpose of gaining relief from the swirls of dust clogging my ability to breathe normally. Calling out for any soul that might be in this dwelling and assuring myself I would steal nothing to label me a common thief, I saw on a nearby table what looked like four or five papers the size and thickness of playing cards with pictures on them. I picked some of them up and on each one was an image of what I considered a peculiar-looking craft. Each image had four wheels dark in color with silver discs in the center. These strange crafts had no covering for above the head, had four sitting areas and what seemed to me to be a glass plate in the front."

The professor fidgeted in his chair, cleared his throat, scratched the back of his neck and looked into camera two.

"I conclude Mr. Corstair was an unintentional time traveler and those cards he found in that house were like trading cards picturing automobiles, likely convertibles, of the 1960s, perhaps the 1970s, a good 100-plus years ahead of his time. Since he vowed to take nothing from that house, we have no tangible evidence of those cards, but antiquities experts did verify that the diary is authentic and definitely from the time of Mr. Corstair. Strangely, though, there is no further mention in the diary of that day of the dust storm."

"OK, professor," Arthur Edwards said, "I understand you claim in your book that you spoke with people in government who concurred with your conclusions of this alleged time-travel incident."

"Well, in my book I do mention that, but I am not at liberty at this time to reveal my sources or what specifics I have been entrusted with."

Emma, noting there only a few minutes left on the show, spoke to the professor.

"Thank you for coming here today. Your insights into the Bridgeriver Triangle, and that tale about the time travel episode in the dust storm, helped make a success of today's telecast." She faced the camera and related, "And we'll see all you loyal viewers in two weeks when we welcome Ralph and Alice Arnold to discuss Rockland Point's upcoming carnation festival."

Emma, with a self-conscious grin that morphed into a glowing smile, added, "You will never guess who will be the grand marshal of the festival this year."

The hosts spoke simultaneously, "Thanks for watching." Then the screen, as it did after each 'Taking You There' show, morphed from the studio setting to a view of Smith Neck Harbor with moored pleasure boats rocking gently and seagulls landing delicately on the vessels.

Did professor Roberts convince any skeptics of time travel? Is there something in the woods of the Bridgeriver Triangle which even he cannot rationalize? Is he in the loop with Hamilton and Manny when it comes to what is covertly going on in Rockland Point?

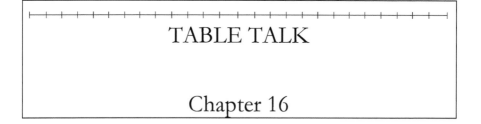

TABLE TALK

Chapter 16

Maria DeMello bent over, took her latest baking conquest out of the oven, set it on the wire rack on the counter then wiped her hands on her apron.

It was her favorite apron, the one handed down two or three generations, spending much of its Portuguese kitchen life in the Azores.

Maria smiled in anticipation of her husband's return from a day's work for The Group, knowing he loved her fresh-baked malasadas and sweetbread.

She would have something extra to cook up, on orders of her husband.

It came about during this day's meal at the breakfast table.

"We have a little situation that needs your magic touch, Maria," Manny said during the morning meal. "The Group wants you to circulate a word of mouth story concerning the Bridgeriver Triangle and the art gallery grounds."

"And just what am I to have people know, or believe?"

"It has to do with the 'Taking You There' show yesterday on WRPD, and what's going to be happening behind the gallery. I know you were out on one of your volunteer ventures and didn't get to see the show. You didn't even get back from the food pantry until about 11 last night, so I let you sleep."

"OK, Manny. Shoot."

"Maria, that author on the show yesterday, Professor Roberts, mentioned a conversation he had with a woman who noticed some activity around one of our portals. She allegedly saw huge tree stumps moved and a massive boulder out of place for no apparent reason. And, she talked about being asked to leave by a military type."

"I have the solution, Manny. I'll put out a story about those behemoths being moved by heavy equipment in preparation for a film shoot of some kind. The Bridgeriver Triangle has been, you know, used for scenes in some Hollywood films. There's no scenery like that in Rockland Point proper, so the Hollywood types sometimes go out of town to get things done."

Manny smiled a knowing smile. "I have an idea how to handle the upcoming activity behind the art gallery."

Maria cocked her head, smiled back and opened her eyes wide as if to say, "Bring it on."

"I think, Maria, you can start a narrative around town about some problems with the aquifer under the grounds of the art gallery, and about some Hollywood movie shoot there. Two different stories. The Hollywood types around here won't mind, because that will take the focus off them so they can go about their leisurely lifestyle, which does include some movie work, without being in the spotlight."

"That's great," Maria responded. "And with two different takes on what's going on behind the art gallery, the public won't know what to think, so eventually interest in it will fade away."

The Portuguese couple had often commented on the convenience of The Group's use of Rockland Point for its covert project. Convenient for being a getaway destination for well-known actors and actresses, directors and producers. Any curious activity around town could be explained away by a circulated story of Hollywood types being Hollywood types or about checking out locales for movie shoots.

Movie personalities did mingle with the locals in stores, on the golf course, fishing off Smith Neck Harbor Bridge, jogging, etc. but otherwise kept to themselves. The general public accepted that. And to those high-profile personalities, that was perfect and they did not care what was going on outside their circle.

———————————————

Manny caught that delightful whiff of Portuguese sweetbread and malasadas when he opened the front door.

He entered the kitchen with something else on his mind.

"Well, the tunnel is well on its way to completion. The route from the Cluff house to the, shall we say, former donut shop alongside the harbor is dug out and just needs shoring up. Now we just need to carve out the tunnel to the back yard of the art gallery."

"Oh, you caught me by surprise, my hard-working husband. I almost dropped the sweetbread when I heard the front door slam. But I'm glad to hear the machinery for boring out the tunnels is working well. Lescontis and his Conclave of Wisdom colleagues obviously teleported the parts successfully to the portal in the woods of the Bridgeriver Triangle. Then you brought that stuff from the Triangle to the Cluff house in unmarked vans."

"That's right, Maria. If it wasn't for Lescontis and Imparo and that island, we never would have been able to take on such a massive project. That natural material they mined to use in the construction of the tunnel drilling equipment exists, or should I say existed, only on their island."

The Group had spent a couple of years seeking a method and material for the tunnel digging in Rockland Point, but all proposed prototypes were too bulky and noisy and would have been difficult to explain away. There was also concern of damage to the ecosystem in and around the harbor, since much of the tunnel routing would be beneath the harbor.

The Group's connection with the island of Lescontis was a Godsend. The islanders had devised their own tunnel digging method. It involved low decibel sound waves, light beams, minimal, but essential, machinery of the island's natural material and a hand-held heat source that effectively shored up such things as mud and loose dirt. The beauty of it was the low-key process that minimized sound, disruption of the surface and the sight of large pieces of equipment which could evoke unwanted curiosity among the masses.

The scientific advancements of that long-ago island had scientists of The Group in awe from day one.

Manny went to a sitting area in his back yard, took out his cell phone and called Hamilton on The Group's secure line.

The conversation focused on Manny's work to construct a tunnel system from the Cluff house to the former donut shop along the harbor and then to the grounds of the art gallery.

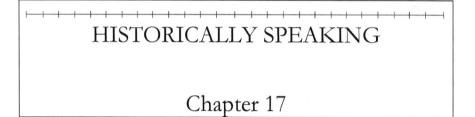

HISTORICALLY SPEAKING

Chapter 17

Manny anxiously told Hamilton how his day went in the tunnel construction process. Manny was excited, sounding like a kid knowingly tearing the wrapping paper off his favorite Christmas present.

"You would not believe how easy that tunnel construction is. I got it complete from the Cluff house to the former donut shop. Those methods we got from the islanders are unreal. I hold a box-shaped device that has an attachment that resembles a garden hose and it emits sound waves and light beams. I point the hose like part at the area of the tunnel digging, move it in concentric circles and everything gets vaporized - don't ask me how because I have absolutely no clue - so there is no need to dump a bunch of mud and other debris anywhere. Just have to be careful where I point it. There is another attachment that looks a lot like a small wand on a compact power washer. I use this to solidify the bottom of the tunnel where there will be foot traffic. You gotta see this thing, Hamilton, it is unreal. The islanders sent this gizmo via the portal on Forbes Island, so we are happy to know that portal works, since we won't be using the Bridgeriver Triangle for that anymore."

"I assume," Hamilton said, "that the sealed-up passageway in the Cluff house basement gave you a ready-made starting point for using the tunnel digging machinery from the island of Lescontis. And pardon me for sounding like a lecturing history professor. After all, that passageway was part of the Underground Railroad in the 1800s to get escaped slaves from the landlocked side of the bridge to the Cluff house and on to freedom. They'd come in to Smith Neck Harbor after getting this far north from points south, be placed in smaller craft to be ferried to the shore near the Cluff house. Underground railroad agents would then move some brush and rocks and walk the freedom seekers through the passageway to the house, about 50 yards from the shore."

Manny felt an inward grin as he enjoyed the irony of the situation. Former slaves going to their freedom over 100 years ago through the same portal used now to impart another kind of freedom, via a vacation, for some of the present generation. Abolitionists then, The Group now.

"The more things change, the more they stay the same," Manny whispered barely loud enough for Hamilton to hear.

"Huh?" Hamilton wanted to know.

"Oh, just this whole venture," Manny replied in normal conversational tone. "But does anybody realize what Rockland Point will be part of? Are those involved being careful what they wish for? We both know the abolitionists and former slaves knew exactly what they wished for, and they went out and worked for it. Now, the desire for what seems like a Godsend in present-day Rockland Point may entail some circumspection."

Hamilton added, "But the very same passageway is being used again. Perhaps the more things stay the same, the more they change."

Local historians were never able to pinpoint the exact age of the Cluff house, other than it being one of the first dwellings built in the town, which was incorporated in 1664. The two-story house on a well-manicured, sprawling acre and a half sported a 1600's architecture style along with remnants of building materials that survived a few centuries of renovations and infrastructure upgrades. The wear and tear from New England weather on the stonework home added character to the white house with black shutters and trim.

Historical papers at the local library did not mention whether the house was built before or after town incorporation, but did say Jebediah Cluff had it built. The designation of the place as the Cluff house stuck, even after the recent purchase by Hiram Passmeyer, who had close ties to The Group.

"I guess Mr. Passmeyer had some clout with The Group," Manny offered to Hamilton. "This whole project grew out of Passmeyer's lobbying effort with The Group. He wanted him and his friends, none of whom live in Rockland Point, to be in on something big..."

Hamilton finished the thought. "...and then share it with the world. Yes, Rockland Point is going to be world famous in the not-too-distant future. Passmeyer didn't select anybody in Rockland Point for the project, because that would have put the secrecy of the project in deep jeopardy. But he has great emotional ties to this town because he loves the ocean-side living and wants to have it all happen here. Keep up the good work, Manny. We'll start receiving our so-called visitors and materials soon."

The Portuguese handyman noticed a friend approaching, apparently just to make small talk.

Manny cut the call with Hamilton short with some hurried words. "Gotta go. I'll have Maria circulate a story about somebody casing the joint for a movie shoot. That will calm the chatter by the locals about all the people flooding into town all of a sudden. The Hollywood types won't care about the influx. It shifts the focus off of them."

This is leading up to some miracle in Rockland Point. But what miracle? For whose benefit if it doesn't presently involve the town's general populace? And is it really a miracle?

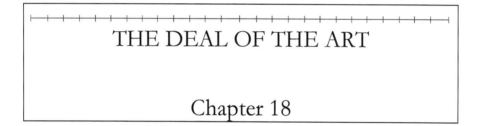

THE DEAL OF THE ART

Chapter 18

The grassy lot in back of the art gallery on Russell Road had taken on a different purpose. It was no longer used for part of The Group's communication system with the island of Lescontis. The notification of the pending arrival of material being sent from the island of thousands of years ago to present-day Rockland Point was now being handled by a simpler method.

That method was simply a stylized 'beep' signal on Hamilton's cell phone. In public, it would appear Hamilton was just answering his phone. If he was alone, the 'beep' would increase in volume until he acknowledged it.

The Group and those on Lescontis's island called the new method 'simple' and 'of great beauty.'

This development of the new notification system happened soon after that error in judgment by Lescontis, who accidentally sent a statue from his long-ago island to Smith Neck Harbor. That happened without providing the proper notification to Hamilton, which at that time involved a signal to be left in the lot behind the art gallery.

Lescontis had been so excited about the progress related to the Rockland Point project; he sent something without sticking to protocol. He wasn't sure the 'send' would work, but it did.

But, no harm - no foul. The unexpected arrival in Rockland Point's Smith Neck Harbor of the weird-looking statue of a man-like monstrous sea creature, found by Woody Engle on a scuba diving adventure, was explained away by Maria DeMello in another well-crafted performance by The Group's spin doctor. She had the townsfolk believing it was a movie prop.

Now she had another assignment, unwittingly cast upon her by the town's foremost newspaperman, Alex Bean, who happened to be driving on Russell Road, and pulled in to the art gallery parking lot.

"Hello Sandra," he said into his cell phone. "I'll pick up the bread and milk on my way home. I'll be a little late because I saw some heavy equipment and some people in back of the art gallery and I just want to check it out."

Alex walked down the path alongside the building and approached a woman, who was wearing a hard hat and carrying a clipboard in the grassy, although much overgrown, space in the art gallery's back lot.

There were a half dozen or so large pieces of land-clearing and excavating equipment. The few trees Alex recalled seeing there lately had been cut down.

"Good afternoon, ma'am. I'm a local and just wondering what's going on here."

"Oh, nothing major," she said in an accommodating tone, not wanting to invite unwanted curiosity about a project by The Group and the island's Conclave of Wisdom. "Just some work on the aquifer and some infrastructure issues relating to the gallery. You know this lot has been overgrown and basically untouched for many years after the school closed and was revamped into the art gallery."

"I know," Alex said. "My dad went to school here. Oh, by the way. You're not getting any complaints from the two homeowners just over the fence from the property here, are you? Like about the noise, and what effect all the digging will have on their water supply and so forth?"

"No sir. We're using a new line of machinery that makes very little noise but does the same work as the backhoes and digging apparatus of the past. Besides, the little kids who live in those two houses are plunked down in the backyards and sitting there with their parents from time to time. We even gave out junior construction worker plastic hard hats and plastic hand tools in a work belt. And also some coloring books for those cute little kids. They seem to love watching us." She then added with a slight tilt of the head, "Pardon my own curiosity, but you sound like a newspaper person."

"Well, you got me on that one, ma'am. My name is Alex Bean and I live here in Rockland Point and work for the Deermont Times. But I'm not here on assignment. I was just driving by and saw all the hustle and bustle and thought I'd check it out. In all honesty, though, if my editor thinks there is a story in this activity, I'll be following up. It's always nice to let people know about improvements to property in this area."

The woman excused herself with a respectful "Gotta get back to work" and walked toward the machines.

Alex walked away, but toward the back of the lot that was big enough to at least accommodate a football field.

He heard the woman shout "ALEX. YOU CAN'T GO BACK THERE. SAFETY ISSUES."

He halted. She approached him. "Sorry. We dug here earlier today and put some equipment in. The ground is still soft and unstable until we can fill it in properly."

Alex did recall a friend mentioning some trucks in the lot a few days before unloading metal fixtures, pipes and what looked like desks, bed frames and filing cabinets. In an open field? Maybe some sort of open-air seminar was in the works. Or maybe some eccentric artist was putting together a sculpture with, well, metal fixtures, pipes, desks, bed frames and filing cabinets.

This was, after all, an art gallery and Alex knew the worth of art is in the eye of the beholder. And where was all that material his friend supposedly saw? It could be, Alex reasoned, hidden from sight in the wooded area beyond the lot.

His curiosity satisfied for the moment, the newspaperman walked back to his car, along the way giving a 'thanks for your time' wave and nod to the woman in the hard hat. He drove home, stopping first at Bakerville Farms convenience store for the bread and milk.

With Alex out of sight and the equipment operators in the lot in the distance, Filomena Bolton, the woman in the hard hat, spoke into her secure line cell phone.

"Hamilton, we need a meeting of the minds. A fellow named Alex Bean was by here a few minutes ago looking around and asking a few questions. He didn't see too much because I sent him on his way nice and calmly, citing safety concerns."

"I know you've been in town only a few days, Filomena, so you don't know all the names. Alex is a reporter for the Deermont Times. He's a decent sort and he doesn't have a clue about the existence of The Group and certainly not about the real meaning of all the activity going on. What did you tell him?"

"All I told him was that the work going on here has to do with a troubling aquifer situation and some infrastructure issues tied to the art gallery."

"Good job, Filomena. You came here highly-recommended by the higher-ups in The Group, and I know you'll do a fine job directing the work under the ground behind the gallery."

———————————

Two days later, a little after 10 a.m. on a Wednesday, Alex was about to drive past the art gallery on his way to visit an aunt. He noted there were no cars in the gallery parking lot. Sensing the gallery was closed and curious as to why since it was always open Monday through Friday from 8 a.m. to 5 p.m., he slowed and drove in to the gallery parking lot. He walked up the gallery's concrete steps and read a piece of paper on the front door. The hand-written note stated: "Gallery Closed Until Monday Due to Construction Work in Field in Back of Building."

Hearing no construction equipment, Alex walked toward the lot in back to check it out. Noting the lot was now fenced in and there was not a soul around, he lifted the gate latch on the newly-placed chain link fence and saw a placard on the gate that read: "Construction in Progress. Enter at Own Risk."

Some thoughts filtered through Alex's mind - Gate must be unlocked for some artist to work on a sculpture with those metal fixtures, desks, bed frames, filing cabinets and so forth - How long will this empty lot improvement project take? - How come nobody in town seemed to know there was a problem under the ground in back of the gallery? - It could be that the aquifer and infrastructure problems were only recently noticed.

Alex promised himself he would be careful as he made his way to the far end of the lot. This area was well past the two nearby homes and not in their line of sight. It was where he was shooed away by Filomena. Alex did his best to stay on firm footing and avoid the churned up ground he was warned about.

He spotted a deer and her fawn not far ahead of him in a wooded area.

Maneuvering for a better look at this spontaneous appearance of nature while trying to conceal his approach, he shuffled through what felt to him like a thick layer of pine straw, almost as if it was purposely placed there. Shuffling a bit harder, he stepped on something hard. He uttered "What?" scaring away the deer.

Alex looked down to see a piece of wood about half the size of a house door. Reaching down to hand-clear leaves and pine straw from the wood, he saw a length of rope apparently in place to lift the wood like a trap door.

Making sure he was not being observed, he lifted it, revealing half dozen or so stairs apparently hastily constructed out of mismatched wooden planks.

Alex descended the newly-discovered stairway and took out a pocket-size, yet powerful, flashlight. It was a present in his Christmas stocking last year. He vowed to always carry it with him because it was from his favorite uncle Joseph and was inscribed 'Alex, I am your light.'

Alex flicked on the flashlight and tried to make sense of what was suddenly illuminated in front of him.

"WHAT?" he shouted.

Then to himself: "So much for material for an art exhibit. This looks like a dormitory. Or the images I've seen of an underground bunker in case of a nuclear attack. And desks, filing cabinets all set in place, bunk beds. And there's a slight whiff of sea water. How did all this get set up with so much of the activity going on above ground? Nobody mentioned enough people working on the back lot to do all this set-up work. Why is all this here? What does it have to do with the aquifer and infrastructure problems?"

His heart pounding, he made a mental note to speak to his editor the next day. Until then, he decided, he would keep this close to the vest.

He took some deep breaths, calmed down and stepped back to the surface.

"Once I get all this sorted out, I'll have one heck of a story to tell," he thought to himself.

Elsewhere in town, a seated Hamilton's feet slid his swivel chair away from his desk. He rubbed his eyes after his routine check of footage from surveillance cameras around town.

There had been just enough light from Alex's flashlight for Hamilton to identify the newspaperman in the underground space behind the gallery.

Hamilton made a phone call on the secure line.

"It's me. I need you to pose as a Hollywood film producer and visit the Deermont Times first thing tomorrow morning and speak to their editor. Tell him, I think his name is a Mr. Whitlow, if anybody suspects a major underground construction event behind the art gallery, it's just a setting for an upcoming movie shoot."

"Got it," the male voice at the other end said. "I'll get a hold of Maria DeMello and have her prompt me on what to say and how to say it."

HE SAID, THEY SAID

Chapter 19

Alex reported for work at the Deermont Times building and, per directions of a voicemail on his cell phone, headed straight for his editor's office.

"Hey, Alex," his boss Edgar Whitlow, a short, stocky man who always wore a starched white shirt and red suspenders, said with his trademark half-eaten morning donut in his hand. "Close the door behind you. I had a visitor about half an hour ago."

In the newspaper business, your editor bothering to tell you to your face he had a visitor is normally code for 'Somebody had a complaint about you.'

Alex tilted his head, slightly furrowed his brow, then slowly annunciated "A-n-d...?"

"Oh, not that," Edgar shot back with a reassuring grin. "It was some dude from a movie production company. I think his name was Edwin Happlewick. He said there is a lot of activity going on out on Russell Road near the art gallery..."

Alex cut his editor off. "What a coincidence. That's what I need to talk to you about. You will not believe what I saw yesterday, not just near the art gallery, but in the lot behind it. Something is going on. Something big."

"Well, I know of something big going on, too. Real big I hope," was Edgar's response. "And you're right. This does have to do with the rear lot at the art gallery."

"This I gotta hear," said Alex, soon to be aware both men were talking about the same thing.

Edgar finished the other half of the donut in two man-size bites, chased it with a swig of Mega Java coffee and filled in some details.

"It seems some movie is going to be filmed over in Rockland Point and several scenes are to take place underground behind the art gallery," he said. "This Happlewick guy is a producer from California and told me lots of material for that movie set is already in place."

Edgar continued with a chuckle-laced conversational flow, "He said he wanted to let me know about it ahead of time so if we got wind of it here at the Times, we'd know it was not some clandestine operation to build a secret bunker away from prying eyes. You know how rumors can grow from a flicker to a full-blown bonfire."

"Mr. Whitlow." Alex said in a ramped up excited tone. "I saw that supposed movie set yesterday. It has bunk beds, filing cabinets, desks, all that stuff. Now, c'mon. If this movie needed a set to film on, why not construct one on a sound stage back in California?"

"I did ask Mr. Happlewick that exact question. He reminded me of that movie about 10 years ago called 'The Friendship Connection' that was filmed mostly in somebody's existing attic in an existing house in, I think he told me, Colorado. Just perfect for the filming, he told me. And for some reason, he felt the underground area behind the art gallery would be superb for his project."

"Excuse me, Mr. Whitlow. But when you asked him why it was superb, he responded..."

"Excuse me, Mr. Bean. But you should know by now that when somebody gives an explanation like he did, you quote that person, but it is best not to pursue his or her reasoning because..."

They faced one another, put an arm on each other's shoulder, smiled, and in unison recited an office catch phrase, "It will drive you crazy and keep you awake at night for no sane reason."

"It's going to be a busy day for you, Alex," Mr. Whitlow said as he walked his star reporter to the newspaper's work area. "First, I need you to finalize some items on our online edition. And I know you're looking forward to speaking to the high school journalism club this afternoon as part of annual career day activities. Which we sponsor, by the way."

"And," Alex interjected, "no rest for the weary. My darling wife Sandra reminded me at breakfast this morning that this evening we will be at Horseneck Playhouse in good old Rockland Point for the play 'Joy Needs a Definition' with my pal Woody Engle live on stage."

Woody, whose wife Barbara would be in the audience with the Beans, had one of the main roles in the play, whose leading character was named 'Drew Brady' and played by Rafael Oaks, who happened to be Tom Cruise's cousin.

In addition to being on assignment as The Times' theater critic that evening, Alex planned to ask some questions concerning the activity behind the art gallery. He was confident he could get some answers since many of Rockland Point's Hollywood types attended Horseneck Playhouse performances, either to scout talent, support the arts, or simply enjoy an evening out.

Was Alex's confidence in getting answers misplaced?

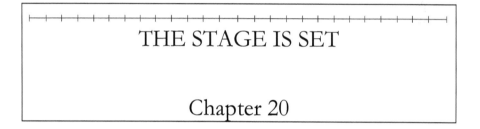

THE STAGE IS SET

Chapter 20

The lobby of Horseneck Playhouse was packed, waiting for the doors to the theater seats to open. On stage this night was to be the play, 'Joy Needs a Definition'. Promotional posters displaying cast members lined the walls. Indistinct chatter by women in evening gowns and men in dinner jackets seasoned the air as did fragrances of perfume and cologne.

This was opening night of a week-long run for the performance that was headlined by Rafael Oaks, a cousin of Tom Cruise. The latter was not in attendance, even though several individuals connected to Hollywood were, but in the audience and not involved in the stage play.

Among the cast members was Woody Engle, sure to get some extra applause from the locals.

"Look at all these people. I'm so thrilled to be in such close company with so many famous individuals, even though I can't name one of them here," said Woody's wife Barbara, who was enjoying the night out along with Alex and Sandra.

"I take that back," Barbara said. "I do know that's Milton Edgehill over there by the door to the manager's office. He was on the local news a couple of nights ago talking about the latest movie he directed in Hollywood and giving a plug to tonight's opening night for this play."

Alex was on assignment as the Deermont Times entertainment reviewer for the evening, Sandra loved plays, and Barbara would be watching her husband on stage.

"Don't forget to be impartial in your review," Sandra reminded her husband with a playful elbow to the ribs and a wink. "Woody's close friendship with us notwithstanding."

"Well, it better be a good review or I will cancel my subscription to the Deermont Times," Barbara said with giggle.

"Don't you ladies worry," Alex said while affecting an aloof expression, cavalier tone of voice and fake sarcasm. "May I remind you I work for a major metropolitan newspaper read by millions, and my standards are above reproach?"

Turning serious, Alex continued, "This morning Mr. Whitlow reminded me to take a positive, albeit honest, approach to the review, keeping in mind this is Rockland Point, not Broadway. Besides, he told me, this is a positive activity by people who have other jobs in and around the community and simply want to entertain folks. He also told me to keep in mind that the script was written by students in the high school drama club. So any continuity flaws, or other such deviations, shouldn't be considered any big deal."

Looking at his watch with the 8 p.m. seating in mind, Alex excused himself.

"I have to talk to Mr. Edgehill for a few minutes. I have time. If you go in before I get back, just save my seat, guys."

The conversation with the Hollywood director would be to-the-point after a casual lead in.

"Good evening, Mr. Edgehill. Looks like a great turnout for opening night. Oh, by the way, my name is Alex Bean. I'm on assignment for the night as theater reviewer for the Deermont Times. Do you mind if I chat with you for a bit? Do you mind if I call you Milton."

"Not at all. Say, I think I have seen your byline in the paper on occasion. I like your writing style, especially when you do those pieces that highlight those people who work behind the scenes and aren't concerned about not being in the spotlight. In other words, like my high school drama coach used to say, 'It is amazing how much we can accomplish if nobody cares who gets the credit.' Oops, my apologies Mr. Bean. I don't want to go off topic if you had something specific to ask me."

"Not a problem, Milton. Do you know anything about a movie set constructed in back of the art gallery on Russell Road? Are you involved in the project in any way?"

"My answer is no and no. It's not a secret us Hollywood types - I guess that's how folks in and around Rockland Point refer to us - vacation around here in your gated communities, use the Rockland Point surroundings as a getaway. But we pay no attention to any talk about movie projects and our supposed involvement in them. It is expected and does us no harm whatsoever. We just go about our days, and since all that talk is about something we are not involved in, it effectively takes the focus off us. If you follow my logic."

Alex instinctively began to reach for his notebook in his back pocket but decided in a nano-second not to. However, he did have another question.

"Do you know a Mr. Edwin Happlewick, supposedly connected to a movie production company?"

"Can't say that I do. Not in Hollywood, anyway. Don't forget, there are movie production companies all over the place, not just in California. I can't speak for every individual who has an interest in movie production anywhere in the country, or places like Canada, for that matter. But I will assure you, nobody I know of in our getaway community around here has any stake in movie production anywhere near here."

"I thank you for your time, Milton. And please believe me. All you have told me just now is off the record. Your getaway community in our Rockland Point environs deserves its privacy, and I will protect that."

"I know you will, Alex. Your reputation precedes you. Well, you'll have to excuse me because the doors are opening and I have to join my wife and friends in the theater. Oh, by the way, I've seen you over at

Paskamansett Golf Course a few times. We'll have to link up for a round or two."

"Hey, that sounds great Milton. I heard the course may be sold in a year or two to some developer who wants to put up a mall, so we shouldn't wait too long to link up."

"Indeed, Mr. Bean. I'm sure we'll see each other around town so we can set up a tee time."

Milton joined his party, and Alex met up with Sandra and Barbara. They took their seats.

Barbara clutched her program and opened it to the page with the cast members' short bios and head and shoulder pictures. She stared at Woody's. She turned to Sandra and Alex and smiled a smile that was close to electric.

ACT LIKE YOU MEAN IT

Chapter 21

The theater audience lights dimmed and there was silence for a few seconds before a handful of the 300 or so patrons in the sold out house applauded softly as the curtain rose.

The opening scene of 'Joy Needs a Definition' began in a non-descript living room that was empty, save for a couch, bookcase and a couple of recliners.

It wasn't empty for long. Erwin J. Snackleberry, a solemn individual portrayed by Rockland Point's own Woody Engle, entered from the audience's right and sat on the couch at center stage and faced the audience. His character was supposed to assume a serious, pensive pose leading to his first lines.

Unfortunately, he could not hold back a huge grin as applause erupted amid chants of "Woody, Woody" from his hometown friends and acquaintances.

Back in character when the composure of the professional actor he longed to be kicked in, he took out his cell phone and punched in a few numbers. He put it to his ear. The show had begun.

Erwin, pretending to be pleasant, said, "Drew Brady, I'm looking forward to our meeting at my place today so we can discuss the project. I know you'll be here in a few minutes."

An off-stage voice spoke Drew's response, as if coming from the phone.

"I will be there momentarily, Erwin. I'm just leaving the convenience store around the corner."

Erwin got up from the couch, set his hands behind his back and walked around the stage living room as he looked into space and began an agitated muttering just above a stage whisper.

"So he thinks all is going to be just hunky dory. Oh, that Drew Brady. He may have bought the estate of his dreams from me for what he thinks is a bargain price."

Erwin's speech became clipped and rapid-fire.
"His dreams could be his nightmare."
"He's charitable?"
"He's happy about all this?"
"Looks good on paper."
"His joy won't last as long as he expects."

A doorbell rang from off stage to signal Drew's arrival. Erwin walked to the door to the living room, reverted to a pleasant demeanor and opened it. There was a smattering of whispers in the audience about Drew Brady being the actor Rafael Oaks, who happened to be Tom Cruise's cousin. There was even low-key applause.

After a nonchalant pause to deal with all that, Woody spoke as the play continued.

"Drew, my man," Erwin said while holding the door with one hand and straightening his tie with the other. "C'mon in. I want to hear details about what you plan to do with the property you just bought. Thank you for asking for my input on this project."

"No. It is you who needs to be thanked, Mr. Snackleberry. You know I plan to turn the property into a place for young people to gather to play games, and develop nature trails and plot their futures. There will be buildings to put on theater and have lecturers attend from all over. I even would like to establish a library and study area. And for those youngsters needing help in school work, I know I can line up some volunteer tutors."

Erwin motioned Drew to sit on the couch. Erwin sat in the recliner alongside.

"Mr. Snackleberry, something like this has always been a dream of mine. And you were very generous to sell me the land at a price I could afford. I got lucky in the stock market a couple of years ago, put some of my funds with it and now I want to fill a need I see in this community."

"I congratulate you on your success on Wall Street, Drew. But I must honestly ask you, will our town of McBain Mills support your project? Is there really a need for it here?"

"Yes, there is a need. Not just here, but also in the surrounding communities."

"Maybe I should rephrase that, Drew. Will there be enough interest to justify all the resources, time and effort you put into it?"

"Well, I have been hearing for a long time now about how the folks around here would love a place for young people to gather for positive endeavors. And I have heard from teachers at the high school and junior high about wanting to put some joy in the everyday lives that populate the area."

"I have heard that, too. And you know what? I like the way you think. I mean you think big. It was a joy for me to sell you the property at the former Everton Manchester farm."

"Yes, and thank you for that, Mr. Snackleberry."

"Well, that's very kind of you, Mr. Brady. And I have made the contacts you asked me about. I can vouch for the contractors I lined up for you. But I have listed on this paper for you some of the changes I think are necessary in the layout and a few other suggestions. I appreciate being asked for my input."

The character Drew Brady dominated the stage time for the remainder of the play. Among the several scenes were:

---his office where he pored over blueprints and made phone calls to developers.

---an outside backdrop where he scanned the recently-purchased property.

---a town hall-type meeting with Drew fielding questions from townspeople about the project.

---one-on-one conversations with young people whom he was certain would benefit from the project.

---a ground breaking ceremony.

There was also a diner scene in which Drew was approached by half dozen or so townspeople, each one expressing joy that the project was on its way to fruition.

"Well, thank you," a smiling Drew said to each visitor to his table in that scene, as he manipulated his knife and fork on a plate that contained real pancakes and sausage so he did not have to fake the eating procedure.

As that scene closed, one of the visitors to his table proclaimed, "This project is what we want to have around here, Mr. Brady. It will bring so much joy to so many people. This is what we want. There is absolutely nothing about it that is negative."

To which Drew replied, "You are so right. This is what everybody seems to want, and this is what everybody is going to get."

Throughout the play, Barbara held a copy of the stage production's script. She was about as familiar with it as the cast was because she and Woody spent hours rehearsing the dialogue.

There wasn't as much dialogue for the Snackleberry character as Woody would have liked, but as he told people in the weeks leading up to opening night, "Rafael Oaks is the drawing card, not me. However, I assure myself and anybody who will listen, that one does not start out in this business as the leading man. One must earn that reputation. That puts some pressure on me, but if that's what I have to do to climb the acting ladder of success. So be it."

The first time Barbara heard Woody express that thought, she told him it sounded corny and she even chuckled a bit. Her reaction soon did a 180 and she pledged her full support to him as he pursued his acting ambition.

Back on stage in the scene depicting Drew scanning the landscape he purchased, Woody's character did a have a line, and Barbara mouthed it as he delivered it.

"Well, here is what you bought, Drew. Look at all that land. Your mind's eye must be busy with images of what buildings will go where."

Drew then swept his arm to encompass what was on the massive painted set of an open field and a pond big enough to row a dinghy on a leisurely afternoon. He then spoke for a good four to five minutes, laying out his vision of what the finished project, which he named McBain Meadows, would look like. It was a playwright's tool to provide the audience with a mental picture of what was taking shape.

One of Woody's character's other lines was in the scene of the ground breaking ceremony for McBain Meadows. Snackleberry and Drew were side by side, holding shovels to imaginary dirt and posing face-forward to the audience, which understood the characters were supposedly accommodating photographers from the local media. "Enjoy this moment, Drew," Snackleberry offered. "It will be a day you have anticipated, and will likely never forget."

This was followed by a two-minute scene depicting Drew on a radio talk show thanking "all those who had anything to do with the realized dream known as McBain Meadows. This is what everybody wants."

Next was a scene of a flock of teenagers thanking Drew for their new facility which had been in operation for just over a year.

There were brief scenes depicting activity at the many facilities at McBain Meadows - the lecture hall, the play areas, study halls.

The curtain closed and the Horseneck Playhouse Theater went pitch black. There was no doubt the play was nearing its conclusion, but the audience's instinct was correct and nobody got up and left. This was not the finish to the opening night performance.

Somber music played.

The curtain raised and the lights went back on, albeit dimly.

There was Drew Brady, head in hands at a work desk in his study. He was sobbing. He looked up in a prayerful pose.

"Why did this happen?" he asked to the heavens. "I didn't read the fine print on that paper I signed with Snackleberry to buy the property. I owe back taxes I can't afford; I cannot possibly come up with the money for the town-mandated infrastructure upgrades. McBain Meadows is no more. I put my life savings into it, thinking I could get subsidies and tax breaks. But now I'm broke. The authorities have shut it down. Erwin Snackleberry refuses to buy the property back, reminding me I should have read the contract. What was it, a contract with the devil?"

He faced the audience, looked into space and spoke.

"I could ask for help from the community to get McBain Meadows back up and running. Fat chance for that happening because nobody cares about it anymore. 'Great idea' everybody said when this project got underway. 'We need it' they all said. 'What a joy it will be'. But now it's not a big deal anymore to anybody."

Drew spoke the play's final lines.

"Everybody cares about fulfilling a dream. Then they learn they don't really know what they want or decide they don't want what they thought they did. Joy? Please define that for me."

The curtain closed. The cast stepped out from behind it, faced the audience, joined hands and bowed in unison to a standing ovation amid shouts of 'Woody, Woody' and 'Hey Rafael, say hello to Tom for me'.

The lobby bustled with the exiting play-goers. Barbara, Sandra and Alex hung back, waiting for Woody to emerge from the dressing room area so they could go to Yvette's Diner for a cheeseburger, fries and a shake, Woody's favorite three-course meal.

Hamilton happened by, said he enjoyed the play and gave Barbara a big smile and a hug in recognition of Woody's performance.

Hamilton looked at Alex as if he had something to say. He said nothing and left for home.

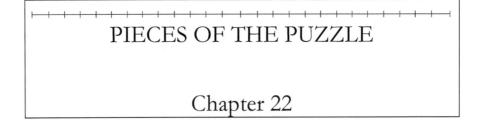

PIECES OF THE PUZZLE

Chapter 22

A newly-found artifact in Rockland Point will turn out to be priceless. But 'priceless' to whom and for what reason and into whose definition of priceless does it fit?

Hamilton woke the morning after the play at 7:30. It was earlier than normal for him, but the knowledge that the covert project in Rockland Point, of which he was a key player, was progressing at a goodly pace deprived him of the ability to sleep.

At about 9 a.m. he contacted Manny on the secure cell phone line. Manny was at Forbes Island, doing routine maintenance on a portal there to welcome a time-traveling contingent from the island of Lescontis.

That contingent would join a cadre of technicians from The Group and set up shop underground beneath the apparently empty lot behind the art gallery. That assemblage needed the beds, filing cabinets, desks, etc., which were already in place to allow the Rockland Point project to proceed.

"How does it feel to be back on Forbes Island, Manny? I remember how upset you were when The Group shut down the operation there a while back. You had it set up for the helicopters to land and all so you could dispose of those now-antiquated teleportation tubes. Then when you were ordered to shut that operation down you had to neutralize the quicksand, drain the security moats and kill the snakes there and basically leave no tell-tale signs of a covert operation. You must be in your glory now that the island's being used again."

"Well, I have to say it feels just great. I'm so glad I was able to convince The Group higher-ups that the time-travel portal in the Bridgeriver Triangle was not secure from prying eyes and should be scrapped in favor of this one here on Forbes. The side of the island where I am now is out of sight of the mainland. There will be no island lights this time because we no longer use disposable teleportation tubes that need to be destroyed. So those being sent here via time travel simply end up in the portal I'm putting together."

Hamilton reminded Manny the island probably would get no visitors anyway, since The Group had recently placed large signs reading 'Unstable Ground and Toxic Waste Detected on Large Sections of This Island. Enter at Your Own Risk' all around the island perimeter on six-foot high chain link fencing.

Then.

"WHAT?..."Manny spewed into the phone.

There was silence too long for Hamilton's comfort.

"Oh my God, Manny. Are you all right?"

"Hamilton. Sorry. I'm just fine. I was digging out some debris near the placement of the time travel portal. I almost had the debris out and I was down a few feet to make sure I got it all, and then I dropped my phone. And you will never guess what I found when I picked it up."

Hamilton asked, "What did you find? Dinosaur bones? Jimmy Hoffa? What is it?"

Manny's side of the call, except for some heavy breathing from his work load, went wordless again for close to a minute.

Hamilton was becoming impatient.

Manny finally spoke.

"What I found is an almost-intact vase, or some such vessel, about a foot high. It has some noticeable cracks and what look like stubs of broken handles on two sides, but other than that, pretty much all of the vase is there. Maybe it was used to carry water. I don't know. It's likely old, too. Hundreds of years old? More than that? I'd like to find out."

After another pause, Manny described a scene depicted on the object.

"There's a representation of people walking on what appears to be a representation of a land mass which is surrounded by water. And here's the kicker, Hamilton. There is what appears to be some odd-looking writing in the lower right corner of the scene. The writing is kind of obscured from being in the dirt for a long time, and I may have accidentally wiped some of it away when I swept some dirt off it with my hand. But I'm sure there's enough of it left so it can be deciphered. Remember, the Dead Sea Scrolls had big chunks missing, but there was enough there so they could be translated."

"Maybe you can figure this one out, Manny. With your training by The Group, you learned, among other things, to decipher writings and symbols. I recall you were able to decode some strange scribbling on a boulder in Vermont that simply declared the boundary of a farmer's property after the locals there were sure it was a secret message left by Vikings who visited North America hundreds of years before. Also, you helped out some archaeologists once with interpreting writing on papyrus by ancient peoples. So tell me. What do you think this writing might say?"

"There is not much writing left, unfortunately, but my gut feeling is it is a name or indentifying information of a specific individual. As far as how old it is no clue yet. Is it native American in origin, some leftover pottery from pre-Colonial days? Native Americans had no written language that we know of."

Hamilton asked Manny to take a picture of the vase and cell-phone it to him. Hamilton liked what he saw.

"Hey, you're a decent photographer. Nice picture. Tell you what. I'll bring this picture to Alan Boyden over at Southeastern Mass. College. He's professor of antiquities there and is pretty much an expert on local history from an archaeological standpoint. I have a hunch this might be something more than just an old ceramic-type artifact. And don't you worry. I won't spill one single word about where it came from. Gotta keep the island portal project a total secret."

"Hey, what about this, Hamilton? Tell this professor Boyden you ran across a farmer at the flea market last week in North Freetown and he had this object at his table. He had no clue of its origin, saying it was passed down from his grandfather who had a farm around here. Then tell Professor Boyden you told the farmer you'd like to take a photo of it because you were curious about it and knew somebody who could give it a look-see."

"Great idea, I agree. And keep up the good work. Catch you later."

Hamilton's next call was to the college. He learned from a recording at the school's call center that Professor Boyden would be out of his final class for the day at 1 p.m.

The Rolex on Hamilton's left wrist read 1:15 p.m. as he bounded up the college's concrete steps, into the main hall and headed for the professor's office, hoping to find him at his desk.

He did. That door was always open.

"Hello professor Boyden."

"That I am. And who might I presume you to be?"

"I am Hamilton Forbes. We met last spring when we were in the same foursome at the annual Seniors in Need charity golf tournament at Paskamansett Golf Course."

"Yes. Yes. Yes. Are you here to ask me to play in the tournament again?"

"Not really. I'm actually here to call upon your expertise in historical artifacts. I have a picture on my cell phone of something I think is ceramic, like a vase of some sort. I ran across it at a flea market last week and snapped this picture. Here, take a good look and let me know what you think."

"Hmmm," Professor Boyden said, leaning back and swiveling side to side slightly in his desk chair with his eyes fixed on the object pictured on the cell phone.

"What's interesting right off the bat is I have seen a half dozen or so similar artifacts or pictures of them around Rockland Point. None of them is anywhere near as intact as this one, but the similarity of blue on white coloring and image representation is uncanny."

"Tell me, professor. Where exactly were the other examples found?"

"Well, one I recall was about two years ago at an archaeological dig in the Bridgeriver Triangle. The guys were meticulously excavating what was believed to be the former site of a fire pit and longhouse, or Indian lodge as the general public refers to it, and about four feet down they came across a couple of shards of pottery, similar in some respects to the object you showed me."

Hamilton asked if he could see the shards from the Triangle dig, only to hear they were never up for public viewing and, unfortunately, nobody seems to know their whereabouts.

"Believe it or not," the professor said, "I did inquire about them six months or so ago and I repeat nobody, as in nobody, has any idea where they might be. But back on topic, I did see some other shards we're talking about that were dug up by some teenagers a few years ago out by the art gallery. And honestly, those pieces of pottery or whatever, looked just like the others. Those teenagers showed them to me, let me keep them for a day or two to have them studied, then I gave them back. They found those shards in the first place, I guess, because they had nothing to do one day, and decided to legitimately dig for Indian artifacts, something one of their dads did a lot of. Again, those kids told me they don't know the whereabouts of the material today. Probably to them it was just some old pottery, not arrowheads or spear points they had hoped to find, and didn't interest them very much, so they tossed them away."

Hamilton asked if carbon dating was attempted on the find of the teenagers.

"Actually, yes. I took them up to a former college classmate of mine, he's on the faculty at MIT, and he gave me some disappointing news. He claimed the particular clay-like composition of the samples made accurate carbon dating results virtually impossible. He told me one attempt could indicate an age of 200 years, and another attempt on the same sample could yield a reading of 3,000 years or more. I passed that news on to the kids and gave them the shards back."

Hamilton called Manny and relayed the information from Alan Boyden.

The finding of the bits of the pottery or whatever in different locations had Hamilton wondering. Maybe Manny would wonder also. Maybe Manny thought he had it figured out.

IT'S ONLY A MATTER OF TIME

Chapter 23

The process of teleporting material and people from the long-ago island of Lescontis to Rockland Point was necessary and straightforward.

Necessary because the island's Conclave of Wisdom needed to work literally side-by-side with The Group to carry out the Rockland Point project that would make the coastal Massachusetts town known to the world.

Straightforward because those on the long-ago island heading to a destination thousands of years into their future simply walked into an enclosure similar to a large elevator car, calibrated the mechanism and flipped a switch. Moments later they felt themselves waking from a deep sleep, walked out of their enclosure and were on a secluded area on Forbes Island in present day in Rockland Point being welcomed by Manny.

It was the same routine for material headed for the Rockland Point Project.

This had been going on for close to a month, with Manny a one-man reception committee. He ferried the island arrivals to the mostly land-locked side of Smith Neck Harbor and secreted them to the Cluff house.

Some material sent by the islanders, much of it packed in containers the size and shape of beach coolers, also went to the Cluff house to be logged in.

Eventually all the arrivals, human and otherwise, went to the newly constructed underground space behind the art gallery on Russell Road.

That was the staging area for the project that would make Rockland Point world famous.

After transporting that latest couple of material coolers to the staging area, Manny had that euphoric feeling one gets when one experiences a serendipitous revelation. The pottery find, the information professor Boyden gave Hamilton and the trouble-free time travel of people and material from the island of Lescontis had Manny sure he had it figured.

What did Manny believe he had figured out? To him, it all made sense.

"That has to be why," the Portuguese handyman said to himself. Here he was on Forbes Island doing some routine maintenance on the time travel portal as directed by The Group. Oh, how he wanted to high five somebody, anybody. But he was alone. Oh, how he wanted to leap and click his heels. But he was in his 60s.

He got Hamilton back on the phone.

"Hey, Hamilton. Remember I mentioned at the end of our last chat that I felt the time travel to here from Lescontis's island was going super-smooth? I mean, when they sent us anything for our project here in Rockland Point, there was absolutely no hitch?"

"C'mon Manny. Get to the point."

"OK. Here it is Hamilton. In order to teleport, or time travel people or material to us, in the correct time element, namely our date and time, and in the correct place, namely Rockland Point, the islanders supposedly needed to, at their end, calibrate both time and location. But, when I logged in the arrival here, the teleportation mechanism I monitored showed only a time element at their end had been activated."

There was a pause at both ends of the cell phone connection. Hamilton was trying to digest Manny's point. Manny finally launched into his revelation.

"That super-smooth teleportation situation I was talking about means the senders from the island of Lescontis needed to focus only on what time in their future, our present, the material or people needed to be sent. They didn't calibrate where it was to be sent. By that I mean Rockland Point. If they had calibrated both time and place, it would have registered at my end on the mechanism I use to log in all arrivals at the Forbes Island location. First it made no sense to me. Then it made all the sense in the world."

The Portuguese handyman looked at the mechanism he was talking about. It sat on a small table and was about the size of a microwave oven. Its three knobs with numbers and symbols on them akin to a safe's combination lock formed a triangle. Manny, when logging in all sends from the island, manipulated the knobs to reveal digital readings on a small screen above each knob. These readings told him what information the senders from the island used to deliver any material or people to Rockland Point. Manny would then verify the material and/or people had been received in Rockland Point. If he detected a problem he would contact the technicians on the island of Lescontis.

But now digital readings appeared only on the time element knob. The other two digital readings screens (for location and verification of receipt at a specific location) were blank.

"Manny, any time today," Hamilton implored with a goodly dose of sarcasm. "What the heck is your point?"

"My point is this. If the islanders did activate the time element on the time travel gizmo, but did not activate the intended location on the sending of material protocol, it means they didn't need to do anything with the location mechanism."

"Are you thinking the same thing I am?" Hamilton asked with excitement.

"Yes," was Manny's excited reply. "The island of Lescontis and Rockland Point, the Bridgeriver Triangle, Forbes Island, the area around the art gallery. They are all in the same place. Over the years, thousands to be sure, water seeped in from the ocean and created a harbor which changed the configuration of this area. But the bottom line is we are on the island of Lescontis."

"So," Hamilton said. "That pottery you found on Forbes Island, the shards the kids found and the bits of pottery that was dug up by the archaeologists in the Bridgeriver Triangle. It was long ago discarded for whatever reason, but had to have a common source of origin because of the similarity of the found pieces."

The Conclave of Wisdom obviously had it figured out. Manny just needed to verify it. The next thing he needed to do was ask a question of Lescontis. A question nobody in The Group had bothered to ask.

The question was what is the name of the island of long ago?

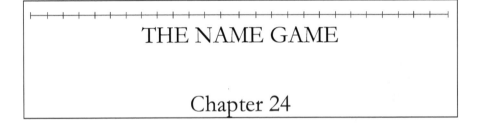

THE NAME GAME

Chapter 24

Manny, Maria and Hamilton were only part of the project in Rockland Point. While they were doing the leg work, so to speak, others in The Group and the Conclave of Wisdom were manning the communication aspect.

All communication between The Group and the Conclave was archived in encrypted form, and copies of it were provided to Hamilton, Manny and Maria.

There was a secure-line phone conversation between Manny and Hamilton regarding the latest Group-Conclave communication.

"Well, here's something I never thought much about until now," Hamilton said, holding his encrypted copy and adjusting his reading glasses with the same hand. "It says here that we, The Group, contacted the Conclave only recently to ask a couple of questions that should have been asked at the start of this whole Rockland Point project."

"I think I know what you're talking about," Manny said.

The encrypted response communiqué from the Conclave read:

Having received the inquiry from you, our acquaintances, and most assuredly friends, of The Group, we are much pleased to answer. These may be simple questions you have put forth to us, although it gives us much happiness to fulfill your request to be informed. We also send a question to you, asking why your hesitation to ask us for this information was so spread in time. But that does not matter; rather we will answer your inquiry to us.

The name of our island is Mar'anadap. The time of our existence as this is being written, in units which relate in your present day, is at 5,000 years into your history.

It is known among our Conclave it is a difficult process for you and your people to imagine a civilization that long ago, as it is as difficult for us to do the same with a civilization so far into our future.

We are, it is established, much pleased to have made contact with you in a place called Rockland Point.

This project which both our civilizations are developing will do much good for many people, although some have disagreement with it. But that disagreement, we have been assured, will be set aside so the project may proceed.

Our people providing work for this project do not use a name for your population other than The Group or humans of Rockland Point. You may refer to our people as simply islanders or Benarts.

Now we and you are one people working together. Our knowledge of the matter of what this project is about is to impart on your population and at some time maybe the population of the world, the ability to perform this.

It is with the knowledge and abilities and camaraderie of select peoples in your civilization that our Conclave members can accomplish this task alongside you and deliver the resulting accomplishment to our people also.

We have had minds wanting to have knowledge of why you at Rockland Point and in The Group's circle of command did not ask of our island's name and from what age in your history we existed.

When our people and yours first became connected by a chance as we each searched for others outside of our own time, ours to the future and yours to the past, we at the beginning of our connection did inquire of your name of place. You rightly gave that as Rockland Point.

You never until this moment sought to know ours, and now it is known to be Mar'anadap. Our Conclave did have knowledge that we are 5,000 years into your history, and we did have belief you did know this. It is now known you did not so we have belief you were more of the energy to complete our project than to place unnecessary emphasis on matters which we understand now are not of most importance for the success of our project.

"Well, I guess that kinda sums it up, Manny. I know you've got work to do, so I'll let you go."

The phone conversation over, Manny rolled up his sleeves, in a manner of speaking, and put his Portuguese work ethic into gear.

The project is nearing completion. The personnel to get it done and the equipment they need are on the way to Rockland Point. It will be a coordinated effort, and Manny will continue to welcome much of the final sending of material and people on Forbes Island. From there, the dash to the finish line will commence.

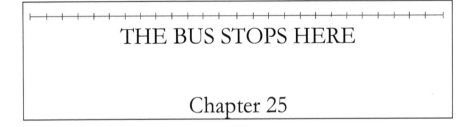

THE BUS STOPS HERE

Chapter 25

There seemed to be much more activity in Rockland Point than the locals had seen in a long time. They weren't hallucinating. Nor were they aware of what the influx of energy was all about.

Certainly not Sandra Bean or Barbara Engle, who were driving past the art gallery on Russell Road on their way to Vadoll's vegetable market. They had to stop momentarily in front of the gallery to let some turtles cross the road.

"Barbara. Where did all those people come from that we just saw getting off that bus and walking into the art gallery? We know it's closed to the general public for a week or two," Sandra said, once underway again.

"Didn't you read that banner on the side of that bus, Sandra? It said 'New England Art Gallery Tour'. So they must be from out of town because I didn't recognize anybody. But I never saw anything in the paper or on TV about our art gallery being a stop on any art gallery tour. Come to think of it, there seems to be a lot more people around town than usual the past few weeks. Like there is when the vacationers arrive during the warm weather time. But that's a ways off."

Sandra pulled into one of the half-dozen spaces in Vadoll's gravel parking lot, turned off the engine and expressed a thought.

"It seems like a nice, well-organized trip around New England, especially with that charter bus, and as they got out some lady with a clipboard looked like she was checking off names as they walked up the art gallery steps."

Making small talk as the two ladies made their way into the vegetable market, Sandra mentioned her observations of the past week or so.

"Around town lately, I've noticed an uptick in pedestrian activity," she said. "A couple of the convenience stores have had full parking lots, an anomaly this long before the summer influx. And our town's two supermarkets needed to open a couple more checkout registers for the unusually high shopper traffic."

Barbara added that lines at gas stations were a tad longer than usual this time of year, and traffic at intersections seemed to have to wait more than normal to clear.

Sandra thumped a few melons, deemed them OK, and Barbara tossed a few ears of corn and some broccoli into her shopping basket. They finished shopping and headed home, while the arrivals at the handicap accessible art gallery were being welcomed by Hamilton Forbes.

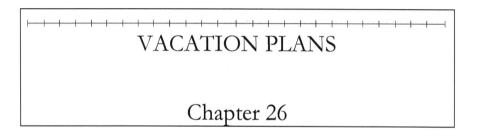

VACATION PLANS

Chapter 26

"Welcome, welcome, welcome...," Hamilton said as the bus passengers, once inside the art gallery, descended concrete steps leading from the building's basement to a massive area beneath the ground behind the gallery's back lot.

"I'm sure you will find everything you need here as you begin your vacation," he continued as all 27 new arrivals, some couples and some singles, assembled in the bottom stairwell. "There are recreation rooms to your right with plenty of Wi-Fi, video games and a couple of pool tables and ping pong tables, a dining area through those swinging doors to your left, a library and mini-theater. All for your comfort as your vacation gets underway. I'm sure Mr. Passmeyer, who I have known for a long time and consider a friend, filled you in on sleeping room assignments with a letter he sent each of you a week or so ago."

Hamilton told the gathering to find their accommodations, get settled, drop by the cafeteria for a light buffet-style lunch, maybe catch a little nap, and then assemble in the mini-theater in two hours.

"See you at that time," Hamilton said, then gave a quick 'so long' wave and bolted up the steps from where everybody came.

Chatter was woven through the assemblage of new arrivals, who didn't have all the answers relating to their present situation.

"Mr. Passmeyer was very convincing when he told us about this so-called mystery destination vacation getaway at no cost," a man said. "That five-hour bus trip is going to be well worth it as far as I'm concerned," chimed in a woman.

One skeptical member of the gathering voiced her observation to no one particular. "I'd still like to know what this vacation getaway is all about. Things moved so fast when we agreed to participate, that we didn't have a chance to get the details. It's probably one of those condo sales pitches where you get hooked into a deal to buy a condo and then find out it's a life-time contract that you can't get out of. I bet the mini-theater is where the sales pitch is going to take place."

"I disagree," said her friend. "This could be his way of thanking us, his high school classmates, for that party we threw for him back in '72 when he returned from Vietnam and got out of the Army. I know that was 40-plus years ago, but he's done fairly well in the stock market and real estate since then, so maybe now he has the means to throw one big party for us. I mean Wow. All stuff is free. Mr. Passmeyer told us all we have to do is be here. Maybe they'll bus us to some resort or something. Don't know where that could be because none of us are familiar with this part of New England. Mr. Passmeyer specifically asked about that when we were approached for this thing, whatever it is."

"We have to consider ourselves quite fortunate," another said. "Remember, we were told we were to tell anybody who asked, that we were simply going on a bus trip. I deduce that would allow us to partake of this vacation without people banging down the doors to come along with us."

"We must be the chosen people," said another attendee. "But is this going to be a sales pitch? Is it just a free vacation that Mr. Passmeyer wanted to hand out? Why us? The only thing I can figure is, since we have all known and liked and trusted Mr. Passmeyer for a long time, maybe he's very ill and wants to do a good deed for as many people as possible at this stage in his life. And since we all trust him, we didn't ask questions."

Meanwhile, up on the gallery's main floor, Hamilton and Manny entered a small conference room. Hamilton locked the door behind them and twisted the knob slightly to check it.

"Well," Hamilton said, "they're getting settled right now and I have the vacation presentation at the mini-theater fixed in my mind."

"Isn't this all so amazing?" Manny pondered aloud. "With that technology from Lescontis and his long ago island of Mar'anadap, getting the space under the ground in back of this gallery carved out was one of the easiest chores this Portuguese handyman ever took on. But somebody is going to have to explain to me what happens to all the dirt and debris that is vaporized in the process."

"It will all be explained, I'm sure, in due time" Hamilton replied. "Or maybe not. It works, and that's all that matters. By the way, thank Maria for spreading the story about all that digging activity in the lot had to do with infrastructure and aquifer issues. That allowed The Group to bring in equipment and fixtures to set up much of what is below us."

Manny reminded Hamilton about the smaller items, which fit in coolers and similarly sized containers, being transported by hand to the site via the tunnel system from the Cluff house to the former Village Grind coffee shop building, and then to the gallery lot space.

"And before the first fixture was put into place underground here," Manny added, "the bare inside space looked as massive as a structure one could imagine was about to become a large supermarket."

The two passed the time until the mini-theater presentation talking about their latest fishing adventures around Smith Neck Harbor and plans for the annual clambake at Rockland Point Congregational Church.

It was time for the vacation presentation. The duo went to the mini-theater.

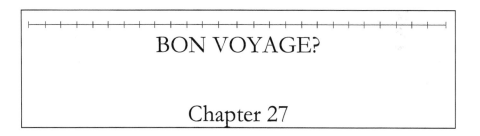

BON VOYAGE?

Chapter 27

The mini-theater where the 45-minute presentation was held is only part of the underground complex behind the art gallery. The complex, all were told, would now be referred to as The Launch pad.

The presentation ended with energetic applause from the 27 chosen attendees. Some gave a standing ovation to presenters Hamilton and Manny. Others in the audience were content to stay in their seats.

The chosen ones hand-picked by Hiram Passmeyer had just been told exactly what their vacation was all about.

They moved single-file out of the mini-theater, some at a goodly pace, others making it a step at a time. Hamilton and Manny looked like pastors engaging with parishioners exiting a Sunday worship service, shaking hands and exchanging smiles with everyone. Some were sobbing with delight and virtually every one of them was beaming with a hearty "Thank you."

With the last attendee out of the mini-theater, Hamilton and Manny went back to the small conference room on the art gallery's main floor.

"Well, Hamilton, I'm so glad all 27 agreed to stay down here in The Launch Pad while their vacation proceeds. They all seem to be happy with what it's all about."

"Yes, Manny. All of them are anxious to get going. Of course the launch will be underway soon; starting in that underground area here these people haven't seen yet, or are not even aware exists."

"I agree. They're anxious to get going and so am I. It's difficult to imagine anybody not wanting the vacation these people are looking at. And it took so much diligence to get things in order. From Lescontis and his colleagues on Mar'anadap, The Group and its connection to Mr. Passmeyer and the Cluff house. I'm still in awe at the technology from Mar'anadap that I used to construct that tunnel."

Manny paused, and then pondered aloud what he had accomplished. "I still have a hard time wrapping my head around putting together that tunnel from the Cluff house to the former donut shop to here at the art gallery grounds. Just where did all the debris go that was vaporized as I carved out the tunnel system? How did the floor and walls of the tunnel become solidified enough to walk on as the tunnel construction progressed, even the area under the harbor which I expected to be muddy and somewhat unstable? Lescontis and his Conclave of Wisdom on Mar'anadap had so many advances in technology that surpassed ours on some levels. But we gave them a heads-up on some things, too. Like how to construct a microwave oven."

"Yes, it was something of a trade-off," Hamilton said. "Not only explaining to them the workings of a microwave oven and the necessary materials to put it together, but some people in The Group passing on the principles of a hand-held calculator to that island's leading mathematicians who were totally mesmerized that such technology was even possible. But just think how all of this came about, leading up to the vacation these 27 people are going on. Was It a stroke of luck that The Group's effort to contact people of a different time collided with the islanders' effort to contact humans many, many years in their future? Was it destiny? Think of the odds. A gazillion-to-one maybe?"

The Portuguese handyman gave a slight raise of the eyebrows and glared straight ahead and, with the 27 vacationers in mind, muttered, "Do we always know what we want, or are we just looking for that feel-good moment. There always seems to be that disclaimer, the fine print attached to whatever we can't resist. Or maybe this time there isn't."

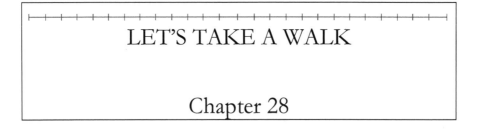

LET'S TAKE A WALK

Chapter 28

Hamilton and Manny, wrapping up their chat, decided to meet at the Cluff house the next day for a final check of the tunnel system. It would amount to a walk-through inspection similar to a last-minute detail in a real estate transaction.

They also decided, for clarity on the Rockland Point project, to refer to the chosen 27 as just that, and to call the people coming into town to complete the project as the "arrivals" or "new arrivals."

Manny had constructed the tunnel solo, using contraptions and methods devised by the Conclave of Wisdom on Mar'anadap. He couldn't wait to show off the next day what he had accomplished.

"When you see it tomorrow, it's going to look like I had a team of laborers working day and night for a month or two when you get a look at the finished product," Manny said.

"Well, from all you've been talking about since you started the tunnel, I'm sure it will look like all of your other projects, large and small, around town. Done to perfection, with a smile of accomplishment, and no complaints from anybody," was Hamilton's heart-felt reply.

"Thank you, my friend. That's my proud Portuguese heritage, the work ethic, shining through." Manny shifted gears and refocused on the next day's tunnel inspection itself. "We'll start in the basement of the Cluff house, where the new arrivals will begin the final segment of their journey. The chosen ones are already in place at The Launch Pad in back of the art gallery and have no knowledge yet of the new arrivals, who will be pretty much the final piece of the puzzle to help the chosen ones begin their vacation."

Hamilton grew a mega smile and stared at Manny who also had a smile. Neither spoke, but read each other's mind. They knew they had done the bidding of The Group to complete the Rockland Point project. It was near completion, lots of sweat and stress had gone into it and it was time to bask in the glow of what was being accomplished.

They high-fived.

Hamilton spoke for both of them, "We did what we were assigned to do, and what I knew my wife would have wanted, but let's hope this so-called vacation for the 27 chosen ones doesn't derail anybody's hopes and dreams."

They bid each other 'so long' and met at the Cluff house front door the next morning.

"So this is where the final stage of the project will begin," Manny said as he and Hamilton entered the house and descended the cellar steps. "The new arrivals will walk down these steps and enter the tunnel on the way to The Launch Pad underground at the art gallery where the 27's vacation is taking shape. Some of the workers will be coming into this Cluff house from out of town by car, and others will be arriving here by boat when they are ferried here from Forbes Island. You know, our friends from Mar'anadap via the time travel portal."

"Oh, yes," Hamilton acknowledged. "The time travel portal you set up. But I have a question."

Manny folded his arms, cocked his head slightly and grinned. He obviously knew what that question was and he looked like he was thrilled to be answering it.

He put up a hand in an 'allow me' demeanor and spoke.

"There will be a huge influx of people into Rockland Point for our project. In order to keep the project concealed from prying eyes of the locals, who will be seeing a larger than normal number of people invading their town, those workers from out of town arriving by car will be shipped in as if they are historians checking out the Cluff house. Maria will circulate a story explaining the many people descending on the Cluff house are there to document the usage of it as part of the Underground Railroad back in the slavery days."

He went on to say that as many as 20 or 30 people would enter the house to begin the tunnel journey to The Launch Pad, and maybe 10 or so extras assigned by The Group would eventually reappear to public view to give the appearance of an entrance and exit. Nobody would be counting either way, so the number of project workers would be hidden in plain sight.

"And that's the beauty of it," Hamilton said. "The project workers, the scientific communities of The Group and Mar'anadap's Conclave of Wisdom finally getting together to send the chosen 27 on their vacation."

"You are correct. A lot of the material the workers will need, like filing cabinets, desks, chairs, medical instruments, some medicine, is already in place at The Launch pad."

The millionaire and the handyman proceeded on the walk through the tunnel that was about seven feet high and maybe five feet wide. They reached the vicinity of the former Village Grind coffee shop and Hamilton paused to allow Manny to show him the passageway into the building. It was a sharp left-hand turn off the tunnel's main path and through a metal door that, to open required hand presses, in specific sequence, of seven of the 26 bricks that formed a vertical line along the door's hinge side.

"And this is where I will break out my pencil and paper when the arrivals are making their way to The Launch pad with you as an escort," Hamilton reminded Manny. "They get their names checked off to make sure there is no breach in security of the project, and nobody snuck into line, and everybody who started the journey is still alive and kicking."

"Alive and kicking? Alive and kicking?" was Manny's response with a chuckle. "My, you have a way with words. But I know what you mean. Security on the project is super tight and has to be. So many people have a role."

The final stop on the tunnel system was The Launch Pad. They walked through another secure doorway and into the space where the vacation would begin in earnest.

Fluorescent ceiling lights above the basketball-court size area brightened the layout of desks, small tables, long tables, cabinets, chairs and stools and other fixtures.

"The chosen 27 don't know this place in The Launch pad exists," Hamilton said. "But they will soon enough. Our new arrivals from The Group and Mar'anadap will be setting up shop, so to speak, and then the chosen will enter..." His voice trailed off as he appeared to be imagining the outcome of the Rockland Point project.

"Well," Manny said. "The chosen know what their vacation is all about. They just don't know who is administering it, or where it will all happen. And I'm sure some of them are praying this is not all some kind of hoax."

Hamilton nodded. "Absolutely. That's just human nature. All of them showed their delight at the mini-theater presentation. OK, Manny. The new arrivals are due at the Cluff houses tomorrow, so let's get ready to get this show on the road."

Manny smiled at his friend, partly to acknowledge his way with words and partly to imagine the joy as the chosen begin their vacation in earnest. That would happen when the arrivals took their assigned places in the special room at The Launch pad and the chosen walked in there for the first time.

It would be a vacation like no other.

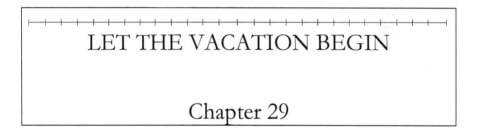

LET THE VACATION BEGIN

Chapter 29

The time came.

The chosen 27 were led by Hamilton and Manny down a long hallway to an alcove that fronted double doors. The chosen stared at each other.

"They kept us occupied in the other end of The Launch Pad so we wouldn't wander up here," one said.

"So this is where we start the next phase of our vacation," said another. "I can't wait."

Still another conjectured. "We know what our vacation is about from that presentation at the mini-theater, but I have no idea how it is supposed to happen. Can anybody really do that?"

Hamilton and Manny motioned for the gathering to be quiet.

"Well, folks, here we are at one of the final stages of preparing you for your vacation," Hamilton said. "Once we open these doors you will notice something special. That being several people waiting to engage with you. Each one of you has been assigned a medically-qualified counselor to guide you along on your vacation. Each of you has a name placard at one of the tables. Go to that table and get going on your vacation."

Manny flung open the doors. The chosen entered and sat down at their assigned tables to interact with counselor/medical technicians who had entered the room through another entrance.

Hamilton stood behind a podium at the front of the room and called for attention.

The chosen focused on him and listened.

"Welcome to your vacation, folks. Just as you were promised. A vacation from pain and infirmity."

The chosen 27 cheered. All were, in varying degrees, suffering from medical issues ranging from migraines to diabetes to arthritis to atrophied muscles to mobility degeneration to deafness to sight problems.

In this room, medical people of the Conclave of Wisdom on Mar'anadap and The Group in present-day Rockland Point would administer a cure for the maladies of the chosen. Those infirm would never know some of the counselors they were interacting with had arrived from Mar'anadap via the time travel portal on Forbes Island. Those from the island of long ago, who would be dealing with the chosen alongside members of the group, had successfully completed a crash course in present-day language so their land of origin would not be questioned.

Hamilton and Manny stood off to the side and took in the indistinct chatter amongst the chosen and the newly arrived counselors. Everybody was smiling.

"Well, Manny, this was a major reveal to the chosen who now know how their vacation will play out. They'll get their treatments, their medical regimens, or maybe shots if necessary to complete their vacations from pain and infirmity."

"Yes, Hamilton. Much of the materials the new arrivals needed to work with came here through the tunnel in those cooler-size cases or was placed in The Launch Pad along with the cabinets, tables, chairs and so forth when the major digging operation took place."

The millionaire reminded the Portuguese handyman of the preparations for the upcoming press conference at the Cluff house to make Rockland Point world famous. He also noted the coordination of the medical expertise both on Mar'anadap and within The Group that made the vacation for the chosen possible.

"I hope this all turns out for the best," Hamilton said, a pleading tone in his voice. "I'll get a hold of Alex Bean and give him a basic outline of what is going to take place. We need a media confidant in case there are other projects around here The Group wants to engage in."

"And I know you won't give him any speck of information about who is involved in all of this," Manny added.

"Of course not. All he will be told is a group of dedicated medical people got together and came up with a major breakthrough. That's basically all that the chosen 27 know."

"And what if he asks 'Why in Rockland Point?' "

"Simple. I'll just tell him it has to happen somewhere."

Hamilton got on his phone and called Alex.

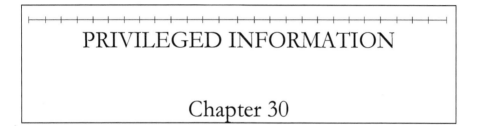

PRIVILEGED INFORMATION

Chapter 30

Hamilton's call reached Alex's cell phone at Rockland Point Golf Driving Range where the young reporter and Woody were leisurely hitting some balls.

Alex put down his club and answered his phone. After the exchange of pleasantries the millionaire got to the point.

"I need to meet with you at the Cluff house tomorrow," Hamilton said.

"About what?"

"Well, I'd rather not say right now. But it's major. Trust me. I'll see you there at 9 a.m., if that's a good time for you."

"Yes. That's a good time for me. My editor told me I have an assignment tomorrow afternoon, but I'll be able to make it if you and I meet in the morning."

After Alex hung up, he stared at Woody, who cocked his head and spoke. "Whenever you give a look like that, you're thinking deeply about something. Spill it. Tell me what's up."

"All I can tell you is I sense something might be happening, or is about to happen around here. I've seen some things around town which simply did not follow the supposedly logical explanations I have been given. For example, Hamilton bought that Village Grind donut shop building from Sandra and Barbara less than 24 hours after they put up the 'For Sale' sign. A legitimate offer, but something about that speedy transaction makes me wonder. Then there's that busload of people Sandra and Barbara saw at the art gallery. Supposedly it was a tour of New England art galleries, but I can't help but wonder if there's something more to it."

"You're not thinking anything sinister, I hope, Alex."

"No, of course not. I guess you could call it a hunch. You know, like what detectives get when they're working on a case when not much is known to the authorities as to what actually went down."

"That's right, my newspaper friend. And like that time you called to tell me about seeing all that activity in the lot behind the art gallery - the people, some furniture, and some heavy equipment. You sounded skeptical about hearing from your editor, Hamilton and others that it was all part of construction for a set for an upcoming movie..."

"I know. I know. And there are lots of Hollywood types around here, so that made some sense. But it didn't set right with me because first the word around town, and what I was told by somebody at the site, was all that activity had to do with an aquifer problem and infrastructure issues. Then we were fed the story about construction of a movie set. Supposedly the first story was meant to divert attention from the movie people so they could get their project up and running in peace, away from gawkers."

Alex looked into space, apparently collecting his thoughts. "There's something going on around here, Woody. A movie being filmed here? A good possibility. However, I can't erase the thought that Hamilton's purchase of the donut shop building and the activity in back of the art gallery are somehow connected."

Woody stared at Alex for several seconds, prompting Alex to ask him to stop it.

"I'm sorry, Alex. I just can't fathom what your point is."

"Well, my point is, I need somebody to tell me what is going on, or if nothing is going on. Hamilton said he wants to meet with me tomorrow at the Cluff house to talk to me about something. Maybe he's wondering about the same things I've been tossing around in my mind. He says it's major. Or I could be lucky, and he has tickets to a couple of Patriots' home games and wants me to go along with him."

The next day, Alex and Hamilton sat in plush surroundings of the Cluff house living room, which had an outdoorsman motif - neatly placed logo golf balls on racks, a bearskin trophy kill on one wall and a taxidermy sailfish on another. William H. Cluff died five years before after living in the house for close to 50 years, and everyone in town always referred to the dwelling on Prospect Street as the Cluff house. His heirs sold it to Hiram Passmeyer soon after Mr. Cluff's death, not knowing Mr. Passmeyer, who seemed too often to be traveling around the world, had ties to The Group.

Alex did not know of, nor had he ever suspected, the existence of any organization named 'The Group' or any organization like it.

He therefore did not know Mr. Passmeyer, collaborating with Hamilton, was the one who identified some people from out of town to participate in the project going on in Rockland Point.

"So, Hamilton, you wanted to sit down with me to talk? Do I need my reporter's notebook?

"You are a newspaperman I trust and we have always had a cordial relationship," Hamilton said. "I know I can ask you to set down your pad and pen so I can have an off-the-record chat with you. I have already spoken with your editor about this and he is on board with it. And he told me he has given you an assignment for this afternoon, which ties in with what you and I will be talking about."

"Now that clears it up for me. I didn't realize my editor had already spoken with you. He only told me I would be going to a press conference in the afternoon," Alex interjected and continued with a chuckle, "It's like they say. Details to follow."

After the sit-down, the two walked to the front porch and stared at the massive front yard that was big enough to accommodate 50 or so people at an afternoon tea, which it often did.

On this day, the yard sported objects hidden by tarpaulin. The tarp would later be removed to reveal a visual aid to the upcoming press conference that would make Rockland Point world famous.

Hamilton had given Alex an exclusive pre-press conference briefing for a logical reason. The millionaire wanted a familiar media contact with which he could converse in the future if need be, and not have to worry about pleading for confidentiality with a media 'stranger', so to speak. Alex sensed this.

But would Hamilton and Alex ever need to interact after this project in Rockland Point? That was not in the newspaperman's thought process at the moment. He just wanted to focus on the day's activity at the Cluff house and follow up on his chat with Hamilton, who revealed there would be a major development, the likes of which the world had never seen.

"You told me only there would be an announcement of a major breakthrough at a press conference today. You still haven't told me what the subject of the announcement is, other than the fact that some people from out of town are involved, the project took a long time to bring to fruition and I shouldn't think for one minute that this is all a hoax. As a newsman, I sincerely appreciate the heads-up and I'm sure it's major."

Hamilton gave a grin of acknowledgment, mulling the thought that his chat with Alex was meant to prevent the newspaperman from spreading stories of speculation around town. Speculation, Hamilton believed, can breed negativity and sometimes sabotage an otherwise positive event.

"Yes, Alex. It is major. Before this day goes any further let me say this. I assure you there is nobody involved in this event who is attempting to play God. You've heard the phrase 'Be careful what you wish for because you just might get it'.

Well, we'll see how that plays out here and eventually the rest of the world."

"I can't take much more of this," Alex said as he and Hamilton walked down from the wrap-around porch and sat down in the shade of a willow tree in the front yard. "I know I will find out what's going on later today at the press conference, but you've got to stop teasing me with phrases like 'not playing God', 'making Rockland Point world famous'."

A crowd began to mill about in front of the Cluff property, seeming to wonder, as Alex was, about the material under wraps on the front lawn.

"I'll bet they think we are setting up for a tag sale," Alex said, hiding his own curiosity of what the heck this was all about.

Hamilton excused himself to answer his cell phone in private.

"Yes," he said to the caller. "I have spoken to my confidant from the media and convinced him there is no supernatural, albeit simply amazing, activity going on in town."

The caller told Hamilton the official spokesperson for the day's press conference, Hamilton's sister, Alvaretta, who would announce Rockland Point's importance to the world, was on the way to the Cluff house.

"It's all arranged," Hamilton said to the caller. "I know you alerted the media to this major announcement a couple of days ago and gave them firm instructions not to set up shop in Rockland Point until today at the specified time. And don't worry. I am not giving anybody outside The Group or not in authority on this project even a hint about tunnels, time travel, and the island of Mar'anadap, whatever. Those who collaborated on this project will be publicly identified simply as, well, people who collaborated on this project. And if I feel somebody is figuring out what is going on, that person will be silenced."

"Thanks for all the work at your end, Hamilton," the voice at the other end said, knowing the phrase '...will be silenced' was simply code for spreading stories of disinformation.

HAMILTON BRINGS A GUEST

Chapter 31

Hamilton entered a pensive pause, inhaled deeply and hung up.

Alex welcomed Hamilton back to the spot under the tree, promising himself to not be nosy about who called.

Alex looked Hamilton in the eyes, man-to-man. "I will explain to Sandra, Woody and Barbara the real reason you bought their Village Grind building. Your late wife always expressed a love for the ocean, and you saw the chance to set up a marine supply business alongside the harbor, which is where Sandra and Barbara's building was. You did this as a living memorial to your departed wife. And I must say...your cash purchase was extremely generous."

"I know," Hamilton said. "With that large cash offer so quickly and other things going on around town like behind the art gallery, the island lights, that statue movie prop Woody found in the harbor, I'm sure there are those out there who might conclude something very mysterious is happening in and around Rockland Point. Of course there is not, but I'm sure there will be skeptics or those who might consider all of this some posturing for a TV reality show."

Hamilton put his hand on Alex's shoulder, chuckled, gave a playful shove and asked in a buddy-buddy tone of voice, "But you aren't one of those skeptics, are you?"

"Yeah, yeah. Whatever," Alex shot back with a 'You got me.' self-conscious grin.

The cell phone in Hamilton's breast pocket rang again. He excused himself again, and out of earshot of Alex muttered "What's up?" into the secure-line phone.

"The package arrived, Hamilton, and is on its way to the press conference."

"Great to hear the package has arrived. Now can you tell me if you have had any word about our special guest?"

"Yes, I can tell you Lescontis has been escorted from the island to our established meeting place."

Hamilton returned to Alex, made no reference to the phone call and filled him in on the media guidelines.

"You are with the print media, but there will be no need for you to search out a place with a good vantage point. I pulled a few strings and you will have a front-row place for the presser at the Cluff house. The other print media may have to jostle a bit, although there should be room somewhere because we're having pool coverage for TV and radio. That will cut down on the crowd."

Hamilton looked at his watch, which read about an hour before the press conference start time of 2 p.m. Plenty of time. Two TV trucks arrived as scheduled in the sprawling vacant lot across the street from the Cluff house, and the radio and TV microphones were secured into the appropriate clamps at the podium.

The print media, a much larger contingent than expected, and others with notepads milled about in the street and in the vacant lot.

Word had gotten out that this presser would be considered "the most important story in years for this area." That label was factual, but not totally accurate. Hamilton and The Group knew the story would captivate not only the area, but the nation, and, quite quickly, the world.

To prevent a media frenzy that could cause a ruckus, The Group put out word of the press conference only to the New England media. That in itself was a potentially massive presence which was abated somewhat by lack of staff in some media circles, travel logistics from far-away media markets and skepticism over the news value of any event in any small Massachusetts town.

The assembling media types, still a large gathering by any standards, speculated audibly among themselves as to the nature of the press conference and more than one guess had to do with what the tarps were covering on the lawn.

Hamilton bid Alex 'so long' and slipped away for a meeting with Lescontis at a house near the art gallery on Russell Road.

"I offer you a warm welcome, Lescontis," he said to the new arrival. "Are you well? That time travel does not seem to have made you ill. It is also good that our Group and your Conclave devised a method of language for us to converse. We thank you for agreeing to direct this language to our method of speech."

"It is well with us for that," Lescontis said. "There will be many more times we must communicate together to establish our purpose. I must thank your scientific and medical community of your organization you call The Group, who worked so steadfastly with ours to complete this project."

Hamilton smiled and nodded, feeling he knew Lescontis well, despite this being their first face-to-face meeting. They had conversed several times through encrypted messages using the communication method established by The Group and the Conclave. They became familiar and even made occasional inquiries into each other's family's welfare, made small talk once in a while about the weather, mentioned they were anxious to finally meet.

When talk turned to the serious matter in Rockland Point, Lescontis and Hamilton often wondered aloud - "Do they know what they are wishing for? Do they know they just might get it?"

That dynamic was out of the control of Hamilton and Lescontis. The Group decreed years ago a covert effort would be launched.

Why was Rockland Point, Massachusetts, selected for the project? Its ability to absorb a large influx of people due to its available real estate for the wealthy and famous was one reason. That would make it easy for anybody or any group to go about business while lost in a crowd. The other reasons were rendered moot in the process.

"I have some news, Lescontis," Hamilton said as they sat on a couch in the living room of the house on Russell Road.

"Tell me what that news is," Lescontis answered as he took in the unfamiliar surroundings of the dwelling which looked nothing like his environs on the long ago island of Mar'anadap.

"Well, the news is I met with a journalist or a scribe as you might call him, to tell him of a major announcement. I did not make him aware of the nature of the announcement. He is a person of great trust among us, and I used his trust in me to avoid stories we would be unhappy with being spread among our populace. The project of The Group and your Conclave is known only to you, me and our confidential colleagues who have taken their places underground behind the art gallery to send the chosen 27 off on their vacation. He knows nothing of our time travel ventures."

"Agreed, Hamilton. Revealing that secret would be harmful to your civilization. People who would do harm to others must never know what we know about traveling to other environs and time."

"In our civilization, Lescontis, there is special knowledge of traversing time and distance, but that ability is the domain of select people with great power in government. Those people deny to the general populace that such abilities exist. It has always been in safe hands because those few select powers in our world do not use it for nefarious purposes."

"I understand, Hamilton. Our people of the island call that 'Providing and withholding knowledge for the goodness and safe living of all.' "

Hamilton turned the conversation to the matter of the moment - the upcoming press conference.

"You are a welcomed guest, my friend from the island, but first I must comment that your attire is appropriate for our time and place. You must have wonderful sources of clothing. Your shirt and casual, what we call trousers or pants, are of great appearance."

Not knowing the proper response, Lescontis smiled self-consciously and impulsively shook Hamilton's hand. The handshake was obviously a common gesture of both civilizations.

Hamilton and Lescontis headed out for the press conference, where Lescontis would be introduced simply as Mr. Lester but not be asked to speak.

He was present as an ambassador from his island of Mar'anadap to The Group, and would appear to the assembled media as a participant in the Rockland Point project and nothing more. Once he returned to his island, he would report to the Conclave on the project collaboration with the Group.

"Thank you, Hamilton, for inviting me to meet you as a person facing a person. The Conclave is much glad in you for doing that instead of doing our communications through time and on parchment, or as you say it - paper."

On the drive to the house on Prospect Street, the two discussed the developments and reason for the press conference.

"As you know, Lescontis, the world in our time is about to start changing. That is, according to The Group, what the people of earth in our time want. I am only following orders as my late wife would have wanted. Is this really what the people want? Is this what people envision paradise to be?"

"People of my time believe it is," Lescontis said. "You and I may be making our efforts work toward a common accomplishment although I am reminded again of our differences in the value of our quest."

He expressed his and his peoples' gratitude to The Group for the bond they have developed, since The Group was working on the same goal.

"My late wife often told me of her desire to have a world with the benefits of this project in Rockland Point," Hamilton said. "In her memory, I have carried on the fight to realize her dream as I have been directed by The Group. However, I will never be convinced it is to the great benefit of humankind."

Hamilton paused to deal with emotion over his wife he detected in his own voice. Then he continued.

"I am sure, Lescontis, that you and your acquaintances have at some time envisioned the joy you would have at a lavish and succulent banquet you may have at some time been invited to," Hamilton said in the tone of a parable. "And, after arriving there with hunger pangs pulsating, you joyfully eat and drink your fill only to lose your desire to even be in attendance at the feast. At that moment, what you once longed for deep in your heart has become something you wish to banish from your thoughts."

Lescontis replied, "There is a common thread between my people and yours. Those being many opinions are offered on all subjects. A thing of exquisite beauty for me may be a random object like a mere stone on a footpath for others."

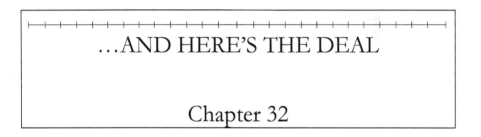

...AND HERE'S THE DEAL

Chapter 32

The press conference in front of the Cluff house on Prospect Street began with the obligatory "Thank you all for coming." That was followed by a blanket introduction of those sitting alongside the podium. They were identified only as participants in the Rockland Point project.

Spokesperson Alvaretta did not identify the affiliation of the participants in the project, that being Hamilton's brother Starling who drew up the plans for the tunnel system, the Conclave of Wisdom, The Group, the 27 selected by Hiram Passmeyer. She simply explained there was "a major medical breakthrough." She said Rockland Point was the central headquarters for the discovery because it would be out of the public eye while research was carried out.

"All you fine folks of the media need to know is that a small group of individuals underwent treatment for their ailments right here in Rockland Point," Alvaretta offered, followed by a sip of water from her water bottle at the podium.

"And by the way, I'll be taking questions after this opening statement. Not many, though."

She continued, "Some of those who took part in this project were infirm patients who relied on things like walkers or crutches to get around. Some had chronic pain from various ailments like arthritis and some had issues such as hearing or eye problems."

There were gasps among the media types, some sporting wry smiles which suggested they considered the event in front of the Cluff house some sort of sick joke, or maybe a photo op for a reality show.

That assumption quickly evaporated.

Alex was in the media gathering, scribbling notes and apparently hanging on the spokesperson's every word. Even though Alex had rookie status among the press corps, his already rock solid reputation as a straightforward, no-nonsense newsperson impressed his peers. They probably figured, "If Alex Bean sees this as a serious news event, then it must be."

Alvaretta stepped back from the podium and uncovered the mobility devices covered by tarp on the Cluff house lawn. An assistant took the coverings off 4-foot high cardboard mockups of prescription pill bottles.

Those gathered sensed a reveal that would fit nicely with a drum roll.

And the reveal came.

Twenty seven men and women walked into view from the Cluff house front door and sauntered over to where the walkers and canes and cardboard mockups of pill bottles were placed. The folks stood behind their former inanimate helpmates, smiled broadly and waved heartily with both arms.

Hamilton and Lescontis, who had slipped away from the press conference podium area, were now watching the proceedings out of sight near the side of the house.

"Well, Lescontis. We see Hiram Passmeyer got his wish. He convinced The Group to develop a program to eradicate infirmities and wanted the launching of the results of the project to be done here in Rockland Point. The world is going to know all about this town and this medical breakthrough within hours."

"It is pleasurable to us of the Conclave of Wisdom and the island of Mar'anadap to have helped," Lescontis said. "We are also of mind to know many times a happiness venture may happen to bring much relief to those affected, only to learn that happiness has a short existence. Our people have long had a saying, which is this: 'A journey to a place of paradise may be more for the love of the journey than the arrival in paradise.' I believe your people, Hamilton, have a similar word message."

"Yes, we do. It is said, 'Be careful what you wish for because you just might get it.' That saying is much known and much believed by us."

"On our island," Lescontis added, "we have had many times of what you speak. It caused many conflicts because the masses believed they were entitled to benefits of advances of our Conclave of Wisdom without a period of waiting. We had a span of time in our history when sources of foodstuffs were vanishing and many of our people felt great hunger and miserableness.

"Men and women of great knowledge in our conclave devised ways to provide more foodstuffs and feed our people and relieve the despair on the island."

Hamilton smiled in acknowledgement. "That must have been of great relief to the island."

"Yes, it was great relief for the first days. But islanders caused much physical harm to each other, wanting to be among the early people to get the foods. It was also of dismay and turmoil at one time on our island when our Conclave devised a method of viewing the future while being in our present time of thousands of years ago. And there again, my friend Hamilton, acquiring knowledge of the future was more appealing than being part of those happenings when they took place."

It was time for Lescontis to return to his island to impart the full knowledge of the medical breakthrough to his people, and time for Hamilton to continue his duties with The Group.

Lescontis had parting words for Hamilton: "There is much agreement with you and our people on some matters. I must contribute the thought that while we may meet folly by trying to change what our universe offers us, we must never be fearful or reluctant to improve it. And we must always have much consideration of the end result of our wish to put our desires into reality."

"Well said, my friend from the far-away island," was Hamilton's response as the two shook hands.

They took a back way route to the harbor to avoid the media masses that were no doubt scurrying to file their stories which put Rockland Point in the world's spotlight.

Lescontis slid a rowboat beached at harbor's edge into the water, and Hamilton gave him a shove-off. As the man from Mar'anadap began rowing to Forbes Island to be transported back to his home, Hamilton called to him, "So long, my friend. I don't know if or when we will meet again." Lescontis waved. His eyes filled with tears. Hamilton, waiting until his friend was a mere dot in the distance, went back to the Cluff house.

He found the area deserted, except for Alvaretta. It was as if the place was evacuated on five minutes' notice. The news people had obviously all gone to file their stories. They knew a medical miracle of sorts was just launched in Rockland Point, Massachusetts. Hamilton had no doubt the rest of the world would demand the same thing and demand to know what was next. It would be all over the news all over the world within a few hours.

Hamilton spoke his belief to Alvaretta.

"This place will never be the same," he said. "Those individuals who got cured have been rushed off to some unknown place so they won't be hounded to death by media people. But we know the biggest secret - that being the collaboration between the Mar'anadap Conclave and The Group. I just hope the powers that be are aware of the saying 'Be careful what you wish for because you just might get it.' Rockland Point has lost all its seclusion and privacy. I'm sure the Hollywood types will be looking for other getaway venues."

Alvaretta, agreeing Rockland Point likely would never be the same, put her outstretched hand on her brother's shoulder.

"I know you have mixed emotions, Hamilton. You wanted to help complete a project your wife wanted so much to come to fruition. On the other side, you foresaw the reality of giving humanity more good news than it can handle. There are other maladies neither The Group nor the long ago islanders can even think of alleviating. What about the 'Panic in the Streets' syndrome whereby people trample each other wanting to get to the head of the line to be cured of whatever malady they may have?"

"I know, sister. There is more than physical infirmity infecting humankind. This whole project has me worried."

Lescontis disembarked his rowboat on the far side of Forbes Island, out of sight of anybody. He would soon be back to Mar'anadap. He walked down a small path he accessed using a specially manufactured key to open one small panel of the massive fence surrounding Forbes Island.

He moved aside a thick blanket of vegetation and entered the time travel conveyance, a contraption similar to an elevator car large enough to accommodate several people or a batch of materials. It was perfectly camouflaged and therefore undetectable from the air. If it was ever found by a curious local, Maria DeMello would explain it away as an abandoned secure storage compartment put there by some long-forgotten eccentric local. Lescontis approached the control panel on the far wall, calibrated a dial according to instructions he was given by Manny a few days before and hesitated before flipping the switch. He thought about his meeting with Hamilton and the day's activities and assurance that the Portuguese handyman would assist the other islanders in their return to Mar'anadap.

He hoped that someday, Hamilton and Manny and Maria would be introduced to the Conclave on the island of Mar'anadap and they would collaborate on a different project designed to benefit citizens of present day earth and Mar'anadap. Another venture into paradise?

Alex Bean bounded into the Deermont Times office, slid into his cubicle chair, began typing the story, and pleaded with newsroom staff, which had lots of questions about the press conference, to stop milling around him and give him some space. He told them that the story he was writing would answer all their questions. But he had questions he knew might never be answered.

He filed the story, and then left for home.

Nagging questions were burning his insides. His newspaperman's instinct told him there was much more to the story than he was told or saw. He thought about those times when he had questions for Manny and Hamilton and others; that time at the construction site on the grounds in back of the art gallery, the island lights, Hamilton's eagerness to buy out Sandra and Barbara.

As he drove toward his Elm Street home in Rockland Point he passed a few television news crews who were shooting scenes of Smith Neck Harbor and elsewhere in town for the news reports that would inform the masses. Alex saw people simply roaming around near the bridge next to the former Village Grind coffee shop. He knew Rockland Point would soon fill up with curiosity seekers.

"One thing they won't find," he thought to himself, "are those 27 individuals who were the focus of this project. They were herded onto a bus right after the press conference and are now God knows where."

As Alex drove over the Smith Neck Harbor Bridge, he slowed a bit and glanced to his right at Forbes Island. He had a fleeting recall of those nights when he and others on the bridge witnessed the island lights.

He took a left onto Elm Street at the foot of the bridge and was now only a few blocks from home. As he passed the vicinity of the Cluff house property, he caught a quick glimpse of the grounds there and the vacant lot. The press conference and big reveal finished and the media contingent long gone. The grounds were all empty except for a dozen or so empty Styrofoam cups and bits of paper tossed around by a developing gentle breeze.

Despite the questions he yearned for the answers to, a sudden sensation of blissful solitude and contentment washed over him.

He drove into his driveway to see his wife, Woody and Barbara at the front door to welcome him. "Ready for dinner?" his wife asked.

"Yes," he said. "Glad to be home."

AUTHOR'S BIOGRAPHY

Dave Metcalf is a former sportswriter and mailman. He had a 25-year newspaper career covering high school sports, mostly in Massachusetts. All the while, he had a few story lines for a science fiction novel bouncing around in his head. This book, "Rockland Point Revelations" is a result of that. After leaving the newspaper profession in 1994, he became a mailman, giving him more time to develop his story idea as he walked up and down the street bringing people their bills and magazines and junk mail.

Dave lives in Florida with his wife Sandra. Both are natives of the sea-side town of Dartmouth, Massachusetts, which has many similarities to fictional Rockland Point. OMG, what a coincidence.

Dave and Sandra have two children and several grandchildren.

Made in the USA
Middletown, DE
14 July 2018